THE BLADON BUNCH

The bank at Pyke's Crossing seemed an easy target and Will Bladon and his sons struck ruthlessly. But after a killing and a wild chase, they learned a bitter lesson — they needed someone who could plan things and show them how to get around banks' defences. Josh Abbot, a scruffy character, became the brains that directed the Bladon bunch. An out-of-work cowpoke and a greedy marshal were both after the rewards on offer. The Bladons were being hunted, and it would end in a deadly shoot-out.

Books by Tom Benson
in the Linford Western Library:

THE TREASURE CANYON
GUNS ALONG THE CANYON

TOM BENSON

THE BLADON BUNCH

Complete and Unabridged

LINFORD
Leicester

First published in Great Britain in 2004 by
Robert Hale Limited
London

First Linford Edition
published 2005
by arrangement with
Robert Hale Limited
London

British Library CIP Data

Benson, Tom, 1929 –
    The Bladon Bunch.—Large print ed.—
Linford western library
1. Western stories
2. Large type books
I. Title
823.9'14 [F]

ISBN 1–84617–050–8

Published by
F. A. Thorpe (Publishing)
Anstey, Leicestershire

Set by Words & Graphics Ltd.
Anstey, Leicestershire
Printed and bound in Great Britain by
T. J. International Ltd., Padstow, Cornwall

This book is printed on acid-free paper

1

Pyke's Crossing was a small town with only one bank, two saloons and a church. It stood on either side of a tributary of the Gila River where its buildings were bleached by the sun and scoured by the wind that raised sharp red dust to penetrate everywhere.

Some of the structures were of wood, but the jailhouse was of strong brick covered by plaster that was once white but had now dimmed to a dirty grey. Pyke's Crossing was not a busy place, and the three men who rode in during the heat of noon were ignored by the few people who were on the main street. They did not pass the jailhouse but came in from the other end of town and stopped outside the bank.

One was in his fifties, with a thin, bitter face and greyish beard that had not seen a razor for weeks. The other

1

two were much younger with dark hair peeping out from broad Stetsons, and unshaven, sunburnt faces that showed a certain lack of maturity. They dismounted, hitched their horses to the rail, and looked at each other for a moment.

'Ready, lads?' the older man asked tersely.

His two sons nodded.

'All ready, Pa,' they answered in unison.

The three gave a quick look round the nearly empty street and then went up the two wooden steps to cross the boardwalk and enter the bank.

There were no customers and only two clerks stood behind the long counter. One was putting money into a paper bag while the other wrote with tedious and scratchy precision in a large ledger.

The three intruders drew guns as the clerks looked up from their tasks. They went pale as they found themselves faced by three determined men. One of the clerks looked towards a closed door as the coins in his hand slipped from nervous fingers and clattered on the counter.

'No need to get yourselves hurt, fellas,' the older gunman told them calmly. 'Just hand over all the money and we'll be gone.'

The two clerks reached carefully beneath the counter, opened the drawers slowly, and began taking out bags of coin and a small amount of banknotes. The noise they made seemed loud in the unnatural silence of the building, and only the distant sound of a bell tolling mournfully intruded from the outside world.

It was at that moment that the door in the wall behind the clerks opened. A stout man emerged with a sheaf of papers in his hand. He looked at the robbers without any particular surprise, and raised his hands calmly as one of the younger men waved a gun at him.

'You won't get away with this,' the manager said in a flat voice. 'We don't take kindly to hold-ups in this town.'

The eldest bandit grinned sourly. 'We'll worry about that when we're countin' the money, fella. Now, let's go back to your office and have a look in the safe. I reckon as how you've got all your best goodies tucked away there.'

He turned to his two young companions.

'Empty them drawers, Nick,' he ordered, 'and you watch that door, Matt. We don't want folk interruptin' the good work.'

The two young men nodded while their father pushed up the flap in the counter and ushered the manager into the office. The safe was a large, green-painted structure, and the massive door was invitingly open. The manager was pushed down into his upholstered chair while the bank robber ran a questing hand over the money that lay on the upper shelves. He scooped the notes into a canvas bag that he took from inside his shirt, ignored the packets of coin, and bent to

4

see what the lower portion of the safe contained.

The manager seized the moment and quietly opened one of the drawers in the large desk. Something alerted the bandit and he turned swiftly as the banker pulled out a Colt .44.

He stood no chance. The bandit's gun went off with a deafening noise in the small room. The manager fell backwards into his chair and then slid out of sight behind the desk. The man at the safe cursed as he ran for the door to join his sons in the outer portion of the building. The two young men were carrying out his orders with grim efficiency. They had all the available money in canvas bags and were just waiting for him to join them. The sound of the shot had upset them both and they were looking nervous when he appeared.

'Let's get the hell out!' he shouted as all three headed for the front door.

They flung it open so wildly that the glass panel shattered with an echoing explosion. Their horses pulled restlessly on the tethers as the three men crossed the wooden planks to mount the animals.

It was their father who noticed something strange. He moved his gun around questingly at the totally empty street. Not a soul moved while the three bank robbers stood as though in a silent world.

'Where is all the folk, Pa?' one of the brothers muttered. 'They must have heard the shooting.'

'I don't know where the hell they are, and I don't care,' their father snapped as he vaulted into the saddle. 'Let's just be long gone afore they wake up.'

They turned their horses towards the north end of town and had galloped only a few yards when a volley of shots filled the street with noise and smoke. Almost every window and doorway seemed to bristle with gun barrels as the townspeople took aim at the three bank robbers.

Matt's horse staggered as a bullet

took it in the flank. The young rider nearly lost his grip in the saddle and dropped the cash bags that he had been carrying in his right hand. He reached for his gun as the horse recovered its balance, and fired a few backward shots in no particular direction.

His brother did a little better. A bullet had caught him in the fleshy part of the right thigh but he clung on to his mount and managed to control the animal as it fought against the bit.

Their father was less fortunate. His horse came down on its knees to throw the rider heavily to the ground. He dropped the bags he was carrying, desperately drew his gun, and began firing wildly at the buildings around him. A bullet took him in the left forearm and another grazed his cheek as he dodged round a corner between two stores and ran down a narrow lane towards some corrals.

There were a few horses there, unsaddled but still with nosebands. He opened a gate, grabbed one of the animals, and hoisted himself on its back. As blood poured down his face, he spurred the animal across two more back lanes and out to the open pasture.

It was a matter of every man for himself. Will Bladon was used to quick escapes. He had grown up in tough mining camps and gradually moved from robbing stores to using his sons in the bigger world of holding up stages and banks. He was not very good at it, and eked out a living that might have been better had he done an honest day's work.

He was sweating now; aching from his wounds and finding it hard to control a horse that had no saddle and no bit in its mouth. All he could think of was to get enough space between himself and those who were shooting. What had happened to the boys did not greatly concern him. Will was strictly a man to look after himself and let other folk do the same.

There were plenty of dips in the wide expanse of rolling grassland ahead of him, with clumps of bushes and long drifts of wind-bent trees. He made the most of the cover, and after ten minutes or so, began to relax a little as he realized that any pursuers had lost him.

He had more than thirty miles to travel. His home was a cabin built into the side of a canyon where water flowed and there was enough grazing for animals. It was a difficult place to reach, hidden by stands of trees and tall grasses that covered any trail. Will and his wife had made it their home for years and brought up their two boys to follow their own way of life.

Will Bladon sat his horse with a slouch that was caused by an old wound in the back that still gave him trouble. It soured his temper and sometimes upset his judgement. He was in pain now, riding without a saddle and with new wounds that festered and took time to heal without the help of a doctor. Doctors cost money, and they might ask questions.

He gritted his teeth and rode stubbornly for home.

2

Maggie Bladon always had food ready for her men. She sucked the clay pipe while she kneaded fresh bread, and the noise she made as her hands slapped the dough shook the table and echoed round the neat cabin. The place smelled sweet from the herbs that hung about the ceiling, and the door was open to admit fresh air.

If she was worried, she did not show it. Ma Bladon was used to the foolishness of men. She had three of them to deal with. All grown up but as silly and wilful as children. A shotgun lay within her reach and a large iron kettle bubbled away on the stove ready to make coffee. She kept the place tidy, cleaning up after the others and managing the house with a rod of iron. The men might be the masters outside, but she ruled her

10

domain without argument.

The lads arrived first, both on exhausted horses, and Nick with his pants streaked with dried blood and a bandanna tied round the upper part of his right leg. Ma Bladon took in the situation with an experienced eye and got out her box of salves and bandages. She cut away the pants, examined the badly swollen leg, and began probing for the bullet without regard for the yells of her victim.

'Hush your hollering!' she snapped. 'If you're fool enough to get shot, you gotta take the pain what goes with it. Now, suppose one of you tells me where your Pa is.'

'His horse was shot under him, Ma,' Matt said as he swallowed some hot coffee. 'Last we saw of the old man, he was runnin' like the devil was on his tail. We was chased for miles until we hit the tree line and got hid out. I think Pa was shot. There was blood on his face last time I seen him.'

Ma Bladon tightened her mouth on

the stem of the pipe. The bullet was out and she was applying salve before wrapping the limb in the torn-up cloths she kept as bandages.

'Well, I hope as you three heroes have made the whole thing worthwhile. I got no more than five dollars in the house, and we're gettin' down on little things like coffee and bacon.'

Matt grinned. 'We cleaned out the bank in a place called Pyke's Crossing,' he said. 'Took every cent to their name, Ma.'

Their mother stopped her work and took the pipe from her mouth. She was a well-built woman with bland, pale features and grey hair pulled back in a bun. She wiped her hand on a towel and gave Nick a pat on the shoulder.

'You'll survive to get hanged,' she told him affectionately. 'So let's have a look at all this money.'

'We ain't got it, Ma.' Nick looked shamefaced.

'You ain't got it! I hope that means

that your pa is burdened down with our wealth.'

'He lit out with what was in the safe, Ma,' Nick said as he tried to move his aching leg, 'but we dropped ours when we was bein' shot at.'

Ma Bladon snorted. 'A fine pair of bank robbers, you two. Then it's to be hoped your pa gets back safe with his share. You didn't see what happened to him?'

Matt shrugged. 'He ran off down a back lane, Ma,' he said meekly. 'And we was bein' chased and shot at somethin' fierce.'

'Well, we'll just have to hope. Now that you've finished that coffee, Matt, go tend your horses. They've had a hard time of it too.'

'Mine's got a bullet in its rump, Ma,' Matt said as he headed for the door.

'Why in hell didn't you tell me?' Ma Bladon screamed. 'Horses need doctorin' just like humans. And they got a deal more sense than some humans I could put a name to.'

13

She picked up her box of medical gear and left the house with her wide skirt rustling over the floor.

'Ma ain't pleased,' Matt said as he poured more coffee.

Nick ignored him. His leg was hurting and he felt sleepy. He had in fact dozed off by the time his mother came back again. She carried two small cotton bags in her hand. They were money containers, held together at the necks by string, and dusty where they had been looped over the pommel of a horse.

'Well, you didn't lose everything,' Ma Bladon said with a grin. 'These was still on the horn of your saddle, Nick, so maybe we're havin' a bit of luck for a change.'

The newly awakened lad managed a faint smile.

'I forgot 'em, Ma,' he said proudly. 'I guess I had so much else to think about.'

She dumped the bags on the table and picked up a large knife. It was the work of a moment to cut the string around the necks and pour out the small paper packets of coin. The two lads gathered at her side as she opened one of the packets.

It contained copper coins.

'You underbrained heap of mule droppings!' she shouted as she turned on Nick. 'All you could steal was a few bags of small change. It was a bank, for God's sake, not a ten-cent drygoods store!'

She threw the paper bag across the room where it hit the wall and a shower of five-cent pieces cascaded to the floor.

★ ★ ★

Will got home the following day. He was grey with fatigue and pain, covered in dust, and hardly able to stand as he practically fell off the tired horse. His sons helped him into the house and laid him on the bed where Ma Bladon tended him with rough efficiency. After a short sleep and a good ration of corn whiskey, he soon felt more like his normal self. He sat in his chair by the stove and complained bitterly that Nick and Matt had deserted him.

'We was in real trouble, Pa,' Matt protested. 'They was ready for us back in that town.'

'Maybe it was the shot Pa fired,' Nick ventured.

Will looked hard at his two sons.

'No,' he said after a moment's pause. 'I bin thinkin' about that, and I reckon as how they was layin' for us. They knew we was raidin' the bank.'

'We didn't look like no bank robbers, Pa,' Matt protested. 'You said to dress tidy and act like farm folk comin' to town to buy some supplies.'

Will nodded. 'Yeah, and that's what I can't figure,' he muttered. 'We was just normal fellas goin' along the main street and walkin' into a bank. So, what happened?'

They all looked at each other as if for inspiration.

'Could anybody have seen somethin'

through the windows?' Nick asked.

'No.' Will shook his head. 'Them windows was covered with paint and letterin' all over. Anyway, they wouldn't have time to get so many guns together. It had to be somethin' else.'

Ma Bladon took the clay pipe out of her mouth and spat at the stove.

'It could have been your big mouth,' she said unkindly.

Will flushed angrily. 'I didn't go talkin' to nobody about that job,' he snarled. 'And I ain't been in a saloon for weeks.'

'Well, whatever went wrong, we ain't got much to show for it,' Ma Bladon said sourly. 'I figure as how all them copper coins add up to twenty dollars and thirty cents.'

'It's better than nothing,' Will growled defensively.

'Oh, sure. You and Nick gets shot up, you lose a good horse and saddle, and you bring back an animal that won't be fit to ride for a coupla weeks or more. Did you kill that bank fella?'

They all looked at Will as he scratched the side of his face with a gnarled hand.

'I reckon so,' he said meekly.

'Then it's a hangin' job,' his wife pointed out. 'We got that to worry about as well. Yeah, I can see us all retirin' to some big city and livin' like politicians who've scooped the bran tub.'

'We did our best, Ma,' Matt said humbly. 'It ain't Pa's fault that it all went wrong.'

★ ★ ★

The next week passed quietly. Ma Bladon drove their little two-wheeled buggy into the nearest trading post to get a few supplies while the men chopped wood, shot a few jackrabbits, and talked about which town they would enter next to rob a bank and retire rich.

Ma Bladon picked up the latest news. As a local widow woman who was supposed to keep a few hogs and chickens, folk talked to her in the little store. News had filtered through about the killing of a bank manager about thirty miles away. The local marshal had gone chasing around for a few days, but had given up when his food ran out and some local lads took advantage of his absence to do a bit of rustling.

Everything had died down and nobody was hunting for the men who had only managed to get away with a few dollars after all their trouble. A reward had been posted, but it was pitifully small and reflected the interest there was in the thieves. Will Bladon hung his head in shame when his wife broke the news of what he was worth to the authorities.

She brought home some fresh bacon, sugar, and enough coffee to keep them supplied for the next few weeks. They sat down to a hearty supper, and afterwards, in the light of a couple of candles, Ma Bladon read to them from a magazine she had stolen at the trading post. Will dozed off in the warmth while Nick nursed his aching thigh. Matt was listening intently to what his mother was reading.

He suddenly raised his head and held up a warning finger.

'I heard a noise, Ma,' he whispered.

'Could be the horses,' she murmured as she put down the journal. 'Wake your pa while I get the guns.'

Matt did as he was told and the family gathered round the window, peering a little fearfully into the darkness.

There was no moon in the cloudy sky and only the faintest rustling of the trees and high grasses. Their horses were in a corral at the side of the cabin and the noise did not seem to come from them.

Will clutched his shotgun in sweaty hands. He listened intently.

'Put out the lights, Ma,' he whispered.

'Better not,' said Nick. 'It'll tell 'em we know they're out there.'

Ma Bladon nodded: 'The boy's right. Are you sure about that noise, Matt? I don't hear a thing.'

'I heard it, Ma. Sounded like harness.'

'Who the hell would be skulkin' around this place so late at night?' Will muttered tetchily. 'We're miles from anywhere and way off any trail.'

'Could be just a fella lookin' for a spot to make camp,' Nick suggested. 'His horse might have smelt the water.'

'Could be,' Ma ventured hopefully. 'Our animals certainly ain't makin' no noise. They're just standin' there, all cross-legged and dreamin' of a barrel of oats.'

'I can see someone, Ma.' It was Nick who spoke again. He held an old Army Colt .44 in his right hand. The heavy weapon was cocked and ready for use. 'Straight ahead by them trees.'

They strained their eyes in the darkness and could just make out the slight movement where a row of stunted sycamores slanted toward the little creek that supplied their water.

'I reckon we oughta start shooting,' Will said as he raised the shotgun. 'There could be more than one and I don't aim to be took by no lawmen.'

He put the weapon to his shoulder and pulled one of the triggers. The noise was staggering in the confines of the cabin as Matt, Nick, and Ma Bladon added their contribution by firing at the uncertain shadows amongst the trees.

The place filled with smoke and the bitter fumes of the burnt powder. There was an eerie silence as they stood, waiting to see what would happen next. There were no answering shots.

'I reckon we got him,' Nick whispered. He moved towards the door but Ma Bladon pulled him back.

'Don't go outside,' she said as she held his arm. 'We fired at long range and we can't see nothin' out there. Let's just wait.'

'I reckon we can blow out the candles now,' Will said. 'He knows that we're wise to him. If he still knows anything.'

'You reckon we killed him, Pa?' Matt asked as he reloaded his Colt.

'Hey in there!'

The voice cut across his words and came from the darkness beyond the window. It was a rich voice, deep-throated even when raised in anger as it was now.

'I know that fella,' Ma Bladon said with a chuckle.

'Hey in there!' The voice called again. 'You sure is the most unwelcomin' kin a fella ever had. Open up and give a poor old man a hot cuppa coffee.'

'It's Uncle Josh,' Nick said with relief. 'I'm sure glad we didn't shoot him.'

Ma Bladon snorted. 'You may be wishin' you had if he decides to move in with us.'

3

Josh Abbot sat contentedly at the table swigging hot coffee and eating bacon, beans, and fresh bread. He was a nondescript character with a shiny bald head and several weeks' growth of greying beard. He might have been any age from sixty to seventy, but his weathered face made him look healthy and vigorous.

He slopped up some beans on a piece of bread and stuffed the lot into his mouth. It was a noisy performance and the others watched as he satisfied his hunger.

'I sure as hell needed that,' he said as he wiped his face with a dirty hand. 'You can cook a real treat, Maggie.'

'She can at that,' Will said proudly. He looked hard at his brother-in-law as he leaned across the table. 'And what brings you to our part of the world, Josh?'

The visitor grinned and pulled a piece of chewing tobacco from his shirt. He bit off a large lump to put in his mouth before offering it to the others. They refused and he tucked it away again with a look of relief on his face.

'I bin hearin' about you folks,' he said. 'You bin robbin' the bank out at Pyke's Crossing.'

'How the hell did you know it were us?' Will asked in an alarmed tone.

'Don't worry, fella. I knows but no other folk don't. You didn't get more than a few dollars, so they tell me. Real bad planning.'

'They was layin' for us,' Will snorted angrily. 'We never stood a chance. And we cleared that bank too. Got away with every cent they owned. You been to Pyke's Crossing?'

'Yep.' Josh nodded as he looked round for somewhere to spit. 'I were on my way to Taranga Creek and heard about it. They was real riled about the bankin' fella gettin' shot. But keepin' their money cheered 'em up no end.

They gave him a nice funeral and posted a reward. A bunch of mean folk in Pyke's Crossing. That reward ain't worth the collecting, so they tell me.'

He spat at the stove and they all listened to the sizzling for a moment or two.

'So what are you doin' with yourself, Josh?' his sister asked cautiously.

'Well, I reckon as how I'm too rheumaticky for robbin' banks and trains, and too old to work for a living, so I've salted some of the old mine workings at Taranga Creek. Might be able to sell a few claims to rubes who don't know pay dirt from horse muck. I thought I'd look in on my family before settlin' down to it.'

'You're right welcome to stay a few days,' Will said without too much enthusiasm.

'I figured as how I might be able to help out a little,' Josh mused as he held out his mug for more coffee. 'A sort of return for your hospitality, so to speak.'

'Help out?' Ma Bladon looked

surprised. 'In what way?'

Josh took the coffee from her and looked round at the others. He knew that he had their attention, and even the ripe smell that came from his seldom-washed body did not kill the interest in their expressions.

'Well, now,' he said slowly, 'you'll concede that I've made a few dollars in my day by robbin' banks.'

They nodded their heads reluctantly.

'I ain't got much to show for it, but I'm a drinkin' man and a gamblin' man, and that don't make for savin' money. But I sure learned a few things over the years. I learned what to look for in a bank before I raided it.'

He looked hard at the three men round the table.

'Now, suppose you tell me all about this Pyke's Crossin' business. Every itty-bitty thing that happened.'

Will was not good at explaining things and Matt did most of the talking. Nick butted in occasionally while their father confirmed what they said with an appropriate nod. Josh listened silently, or as silently as his moving jaw permitted.

'So you see, we did everythin' right,' Matt said as his brother and father nodded agreement. 'We was just unlucky.'

'Unlucky, hell!' Josh exploded. 'You walked into a trap. If you'd scouted that town first, you'd have known what to expect. They was layin' for you. Took you for a bunch of rubes.'

Will jumped up from his chair. 'I was right all along,' he cried. 'That's what I bin saying. But how was they layin' for us? It don't make sense.'

Josh grinned.

'Did you hear a bell ringing?' he asked.

'A bell?' Will sat down again. 'I didn't hear no bell.'

'I did, Pa,' Nick said eagerly. 'It was like a go-to-meetin' sort of bell.'

'So what the hell has a bell got to do with it?' Ma Bladon asked as she relit her neglected pipe.

'Well, these money-lendin' fellas is

learnin' things,' Josh explained. 'They bin robbed too many times, so now they're settin' traps for us poor folks. That bank in Pyke's Crossin' had a small bell up on the back wall. The rope went down to a pedal under the counter, and when you entered the bank, one of them clerk fellas just pushed up and down on that pedal with his foot. Like he was stitchin' a pair of pants. All the folk around town heard it, and the marshal had time to get 'em organized.'

Will slapped the table angrily with his fist.

'That ain't honest,' he cried. 'We coulda been killed.'

'That was the idea behind it,' Josh chuckled. 'You was lucky to get away as well as you did. Truth is that them folks was more nervous than you was. To hear 'em talk now in the saloon, you'd think they defeated the whole Yankee army. The truth is, though, they was scared to hell and couldn't shoot straight.'

'You sure nosed around Pyke's Crossing,' Ma Bladon said.

'Of course I did. I looked at the bank, listened to their high-falutin' tales, and got me a few drinks in the saloon. I learned things, and it gave me an idea.'

'And what would that be?' Will asked suspiciously.

'Well, suppose I was to be a sorta scout for you.' Josh suggested. 'I go into a town, check on the bank, and get all the information you need. That way, you'd stand a better chance.'

There was silence round the table as they all thought about the idea. Will looked at his wife and she gave him a very slight nod.

'Got any particular place in mind?' he asked his visitor.

'As a matter of fact, I have. There's a little place called Maverton just south of Tucson. A real hick town that only needs one bank. I'll ride in there, check it out, and then we make a plan to take it. How about that?'

Will scratched his chin noisily.

'That's near to seventy miles away,' he said dubiously. 'What do you reckon, Ma?'

He looked at his wife for help as she sat drawing on the old pipe.

'The further from here, the better,' she said thoughtfully. 'A sensible bird don't foul its own nest. But why did you pick on Maverton, Josh?'

Her brother grinned. 'They got a stone quarry nearby,' he said, 'and the money to pay the workers arrives every two weeks. Over three thousand dollars. That's worth pickin' up.'

'And you'll check out the bank?' Ma Bladon mused.

'I will indeed, Maggie. I'll do it all soldier-like with a plan of the town, and all the details about the way the marshal runs the place.'

'And you'll want an equal share?' Will asked suspiciously.

'Oh, no.' Josh shook his head firmly. 'I want one thousand dollars. Regardless of what you get.'

Maggie Bladon looked at him. 'Why

a thousand?' she asked.

'Because Will's gonna cheat me on shares. He's a bank robber. So I want a fixed amount. I get one thousand dollars for every job I set up.'

Will shook his head angrily. 'You said there'll only by three thousand dollars in the bank.'

'I said that the stone quarry payroll was three thousand. You don't aim to leave the rest of the money behind, do you?'

'Oh, yeah. I see what you mean. You got yourself a deal.'

He reached out a hand across the table.

'Now suppose we drink to it,' Josh suggested as he smacked his lips.

The jug of corn mash came out and the arrangement was sealed in the traditional way. Josh fell out of his chair a couple of hours later.

★   ★   ★

He left the next morning, slouched over his horse and waving a slightly shaky hand as he steered the animal through the bushes and down the canyon to the open land that stretched greenly to the foothills below the tree line.

Josh Abbot was still too bemused by the previous evening's drinking to notice the man who sat silently among the trees and watched him go.

Mike Wade had trailed him from Pyke's Crossing. It was just a hunch, but the young ex-cowhand had a feeling that Josh was a little more than a shuffling drunk who just happened to wander into town by accident. The man had been asking too many questions in the saloon, and although drinking heavily, he had loosened a few tongues and had listened more than he talked.

Mike Wade was broke. His job at the Double S had folded when cattle prices dropped earlier in the year. All that he had managed to do since was a few odd chores for local ranches and timber companies. Nobody wanted permanent hands and he was competing with older and more experienced men.

Pyke's Crossing had been talking of the bank raid when Mike had arrived there for a few day's work at a nearby haulage business. He had gone into town one evening for a rare chance of a glass of beer. And it was there that he saw Josh Abbot. There was something shifty about the man and the way he talked of the raid to folks who saw it or took part in the shooting. Mike had watched him leave the saloon to go along to the bank. The rough-looking stranger had walked round to the side of the building, inspecting it carefully, almost as though he were planning another raid himself.

It also occured to Mike that the man might be after the reward. Two hundred dollars seemed a lot of money to the ex-cowpoke.

It would keep him in food for six months or more. Maybe the smelly, ragged fella was thinking along the same lines. Mike was tall and slim, with a slightly crooked nose and fair hair that had bleached in the sun. He rode a pony that badly needed re-shoeing, and the gun at his side was an early Colt .45 with a lot of the finish rubbed off.

He could use it though. Experience on the range and dealing with rustlers had taught him a few things. He was interested now in this odd character who had left town and headed for a small canyon some thirty miles away. It was part curiosity, part instinct that prompted Mike to follow him. He had been surprised to find him visiting a cabin there. Surprised that such a place could even exist in so isolated a spot.

Mike spent all night among the trees that lined the route to the cabin. He shivered in the chill wind as he watched the candles go out in the warmth of the little building while the inhabitants slept after a rather noisy drinking session.

He was barely awake when the scruffy man emerged the next morning and saddled his horse. The others waved a farewell to him as he set off towards the north, skirting the trees where Mike was watching. The young cowpoke had to make a decision; to follow the man who was leaving or to go back to Pyke's Crossing with the news. The three men at the cabin fitted the description of the bank robbers. He made up his mind, and followed the man on the horse.

4

Marshal Bob Payne of Pyke's Crossing was a large man whose ruddy face and veined nose showed his liking for an occasional drink. He sprawled in his office chair, reading a tattered copy of Beadle's Dime Library magazine. The morning was clear and cool and the town was quiet after the recent bank robbery and a little rustling up north. There was nothing that the marshal could do about either case, and that suited him. He preferred an idle life. Dealing with drunks was easier than chasing after bank robbers and rustlers who could get lost in the vast spaces.

He was a little annoyed when the door opened and a slim young man came in, shaking trail dust off his worn clothes.

'And what can I do for you, fella?' the marshal asked suspiciously.

'I think I got me a line on them fellas that robbed your bank, Marshal,' the young man said with a quiet smile.

Bob Payne sat up in his chair and let the magazine drop on to the floor.

'Is that a fact now?' he asked. 'And who are you?'

Mike Wade explained how he had stumbled across the cabin in the canyon while he was on his way to a job up north. The three men there fitted the descriptions of the bank robbers but he had been unable to turn back to Pyke's Crossing in case he lost the job he was seeking.

'And now you've been fired and come back to try and get the reward?' the marshal said slowly.

'I reckon so,' Mike agreed. 'I could sure use the money.'

'So could we all,' the lawman answered drily. 'Now, let me get this straight, lad. You saw these three fellas and a woman at the cabin? How long ago was that?'

'Well, it would be about three weeks ago, I reckon.'

'Then I reckon as how they're well gone by now. If you'd come straight back to town, we might have caught them. But three weeks!'

Mike grimaced. 'It was like I said, Marshal. I had a job to go to and I needed it real bad. If it's any help, them folks seemed real settled in. They had a few hogs, some chickens, and the woman to look after the place. It appeared a real permanent sort of set-up to me. And well off the trail.'

'And you just found it by accident?' The lawman's tone was still hostile.

Mike grinned modestly. 'Well, that ain't quite the truth, I guess. My horse really smelt it out. He was thirsty and there's a creek flows through the canyon.'

'That figures. I didn't reckon you for a great Indian tracker. You just ain't got the experience.'

The marshal looked the young man carefully up and down. Then he made up his mind.

'Now, I'll tell you how we're gonna play this, lad,' he said. 'You go eat and rest up a little. Tend your horse and come back here a couple of hours before dawn. Don't say a word about this to any of the folk in town. If these fellas ain't at the cabin, we could look damned fools. I ain't keen to be laughed at. I gotta live around here. You understand me, boy?'

Mike nodded. 'Yes, Marshal,' he answered. 'Are you makin' up a posse?'

'Like hell I am. As I said, this might be a hole without a jackrabbit in it. Besides, that reward will go better between two of us. You can use that gun you're carrying, I hope?'

'Sure can, Marshal.'

'Good. We'll tote a couple of Winchesters and shotguns. I figure as how a brave young fella like you and an experienced old hand like me can take three bandits holed up in a cabin. Are you game?'

Mike grinned. 'Sure am.'

40

'Then be back here two hours before dawn.'

★ ★ ★

They set off in the chill of the early morning. The marshal had added a mule to the little party. It was laden with the food they might need and carried something else that the lawman did not mention.

The sun was up when they reached the canyon. Marshal Payne ordered Mike to tether the animals amid some cholla cacti and then led the way on foot. They moved quietly through the bushes and low masses of yellow opuntia, following the narrow creek until the cabin came in sight.

'I ain't been here for years,' the lawman said quietly. 'Old Phil Taylor had a coupla claims in the canyon but never did find anythin' worth a damn. See any sign of life?'

They peered through the bushes at the silent building, but all that could be

41

discerned in the early light were the figures of two horses in the corral. As they watched and listened, a sudden wisp of smoke appeared from the iron stove pipe. Somebody was lighting up to make some breakfast. The marshal looked at Mike and gave a satisfied grin.

'You was right, fella,' he said happily. 'We got them sure as shooting.'

As he spoke, there was a slight noise from some way down the canyon. The lawman raised an eyebrow and listened carefully.

'I may be wrong,' he whispered, 'but that sounds like cattle to me. Just round that bend. Stay here while I go take a look.'

'Can you get past the cabin without bein' seen, Marshal?' Mike asked.

'Sure, I'll stick to the wall and keep the mesquite between me and any nosey fellas that come out lookin' for trouble. If anybody does spot me, start shootin' and keep 'em in the cabin. We want them all together.'

He moved off while Mike watched anxiously. For all his size, the lawman slipped silently away and did not even seem to disturb the undergrowth as he slunk along the canyon. He was soon lost to view among the mesquite that lined the reddish walls. Mike kept his eyes on the cabin. Smoke was coming from the stovepipe in white streams now, and he could smell bacon in the still air. The horses in the corral moved restlessly as if they scented the intruders.

Mike hardly heard the marshal returning. The man suddenly appeared at his side, breathing heavily but with a slight grin on his face.

'They been rustlin' as well, fella,' he said softly. 'Walt Perry came to town a coupla weeks back to tell me that forty or so of his herd was missing. They're back there, penned in the canyon, and some of the brands have already been changed. We got 'em to rights, boy, and no mistaking.'

'What do we do next then, Marshal?'

Mike asked eagerly.

'Well, I'll tell you, lad. I don't aim to be no hero. There's some sticks of blastin' powder on that mule back there, and I aim to use 'em if we have to. I only need one of them fellas alive for a trial. The rest don't matter, but folks in town always like a hanging, and they did kill that money-lendin' fella. I'll go get the blastin' powder and then we'll call on 'em to come out. They won't do it. Them folks never does. So they'll start shootin' and we'll just keep down and let 'em get on with it. Then I'll toss one stick over near the door. That'll scare 'em to hell and they'll throw out their guns pretty pronto. When they come through the door, you shoot one and I'll shoot another. That'll make the third one easier to get back to town.'

'There's a woman there as well, Marshal.'

'Yeah, so you said. My guess is that she'll be as busy with a gun as the rest of them. She'll just have to take her chance.'

Mike looked towards the horses in the corral.

'There's another thing, Marshal,' he said. 'Were there any cow ponies among the cattle back there?'

'No. Why?'

'Well, when I was here last, there were three ridin' horses and a mule. There was also a two-wheeled gig at the side of the cabin.'

The lawman thought it over for a moment as he scratched his chin noisily.

'You figure as how some of 'em ain't at home?' he asked.

'I reckon not.'

'Could make it easier. Folks back in Pyke's Crossin' don't have to know how many we killed. That mayor is one mean man. He might not pay the reward if he thinks we missed out on some of 'em. And he only needs one for a hanging. Hangings cost money.'

He winked at Mike. 'You follow me?' he asked.

The young man nodded. 'I don't aim

to miss out on any part of that reward,' he agreed.

'Good man. I'll go get that blastin' powder.'

The marshal hurried off to the mouth of the canyon while Mike remained peering through the mesquite. The cabin door was still closed but there was now a smell of coffee in the air. The young watcher checked the Winchester he was carrying as he waited for something to happen.

It took him by surprise when it did. The cabin door opened and a young man stepped into the open. He was carrying a wooden pail and started to move towards the creek for some water. He stopped suddenly in his tracks and stood as though listening. He put the bucket down quietly as one hand went to the gun at his belt. He stared round the canyon before moving backwards towards the cabin again.

Something had alerted him but Mike could not sort out what it might be. He kept perfectly still behind the mesquite clumps as the man reached the cabin door. Then he heard what had warned the young fellow of an alien presence. The marshal's mule was bugling in the unmistakable way of an animal that has smelt water. Mike cursed and aimed the Winchester as the man dived for safety behind the wooden walls.

The shot echoed round the canyon and he saw chips fly from the lintel as the man vanished from sight and slammed the door behind him. Another shot quickly answered the one he had fired. A bullet passed through the mesquite and showered Mike with dust as he ducked instinctively. Somebody was at the window, shooting through the sacking that covered the gap. He ejected the cartridge case from the carbine and fired again. His shot passed through the window and was answered by the blast of a shotgun. The range was too great to be effective but the pellets lashed among the bushes and one caught Mike in the back of the left hand.

He heard a noise behind him and saw the figure of the marshal crawling among the bushes and low trees to reach his side. The man was carrying a small sack.

'What the hell started all this?' the man asked as he kneeled behind the mesquite and placed his burden on the ground.

Mike told him and the lawman nodded resignedly. There were more shots coming from the cabin now but the two watchers were well enough protected in their position. A ricochet from the rock wall was their greatest danger, but most of the bullets simply flattened and fell to the ground.

The marshal took out a stick of blasting powder. He pushed the length of fuse into it and searched his waistcoat pocket for a Vesta box. Mike watched him uneasily.

He lit it during a lull in the firing, and the noise of the scraping Vesta seemed chillingly loud in the confined space.

'Give 'em a few blasts from the Winchester to keep their heads down,' Marshal Payne said as he watched the fuse begin to splutter.

Mike did as he was told, pulling back the loading lever and releasing the trigger until the weapon was empty. He saw the stick fly through the air and ducked as did the man at his side. There was a short delay and then a deafening explosion as the blast rattled the door of the cabin and threw up a curtain of muck and pebbles.

It was followed by a silence that was only disturbed by the noise the cattle began to make at the far end of the canyon. They had been disturbed by all the activity and were beginning to make their displeasure audible.

The marshal cupped his hands to his mouth and shouted across to the men in the cabin.

'You fellas in there!' he bellowed. 'I'm the marshal of Pyke's Crossin' and I figure on takin' you in for a trial. You can either come outa there peaceful-like, or we can throw in a few more sticks of blastin' powder. Me and my deputies here ain't playin' games. Toss out your guns and come out with your hands where we can see 'em. You ain't got no choice. We can blow you out or wait you out. It's up to you.'

Nothing happened. The men in the cabin were silent as the lawman and Mike Wade waited for the next move.

'Do you think they'll come runnin' out to get to their horses?' Mike asked.

'No, they won't risk that,' Marshal Payne replied confidently. 'They're thinkin' things out right now; wonderin' what chances they have if we put 'em on trial. Their horses ain't much use to 'em. They got no saddles and we'd shoot 'em down before they even got that corral gate open. Don't worry, lad. We have them critters dead to rights. Their guns will come flyin' through the door any minute now. And remember, we only need one alive.'

As the marshal spoke, a hand appeared at the little window and tore aside the curtain of old sacking.

'Here we go,' the lawman chuckled grimly. 'What did I tell you, fella?'

His air of triumph was cut short by an object that came flying through the window to shatter on the ground some yards ahead of the two watchers. It was an oil lamp. Its container was of glass, and the lamp was not only lit, but had a piece of cloth wrapped round it, which was also alight. It burst with a flash of orange flame that licked at the dry grass in front of the mesquite bushes and set fire to the lower branches. The lawman cursed as he fell backwards in alarm. Mike did the same. Both men were taken completely by surprise at the sudden turn of events.

The mesquite, dry and brittle round the edges, began to flare up angrily amid a pall of blackish smoke.

'They're makin' for the horses!' the marshal shouted as he ran round the edge of the burning clumps and opened fire on two men who had left the cabin and were halfway to the corral. One of them turned to fire back, stumbling as he did so. The marshal's second shot caught him in the leg and he sprawled on the ground. The pistol fell from his grasp.

His companion had reached the corral and was busy trying to grab the noseband of one of the horses. The animal was already nervous at the sight of the flames and the explosions. The man swore as he struggled to mount the frightened beast.

Mike levelled the Winchester and fired a single shot. It took the rider in the chest and he tumbled from the horse. The other man had recovered his pistol and rolled over on the ground to fire on the advancing marshal. The lawman saw the move and pulled the trigger as he dodged to one side. His shot hit the man in the side of the neck. He dropped the gun and lay still.

Marshal Payne and Mike Wade stood side by side looking down at the two figures. They were young men, unshaven but neatly dressed. Their hair was dark above tanned faces and both had long sideburns.

'They ain't the fellas as was here with the woman,' Mike said uneasily. 'Nothin' like 'em, Marshal.'

The lawman slapped his thigh angrily. 'They certainly ain't, son,' he complained bitterly. 'These two no-goods are Ma Kent's boys. Two cheap thieves who ain't worth a Confederate dollar. Stealin' a few head of cattle is all they're fit for. We got the wrong ones, I reckon, but at least the town will be pleased to know we've rid them of a few more coyotes. Let's take a look in the cabin.'

He led the way to the little building and stood in the middle of the single room, looking around at its surprising neatness.

'Sure got a woman's touch,' he said as he crossed to the stove where the bacon and coffee were still keeping hot. 'I reckon as how the folks who was here when you came across the cabin, have lit out. These fellas needed a hidin' place for what they'd stole, so they just moved in. We got ourselves some breakfast, if nothin' else. Then you can help me get these dead 'uns back to town and be on your way, wherever you're going.'

He raised an eyebrow as he spoke, as if the last words were a question.

'I gotta find another job,' Mike said quietly. 'Ain't got more than a coupla dollars to my name.'

The lawman grinned as he picked up the coffee pot.

'There's two horses out there,' he said, 'and a coupla saddles. Then there's their guns. You'll get your share of that. So don't worry about eatin' for the next week or two.'

'Thanks, Marshal. I sure wish it had been them bank robbers, though.'

'So do I, son. So do I. But don't worry. They'll slip up some day. You can lay odds on that.'

5

It was all Ma Bladon's doing. After her brother departed in a still-inebriated state, she had set about her usual chores while the men went out with shotguns to nab a few jackrabbits for the pot. As she was searching for eggs in the usual places her hens chose to lay them, she came upon fresh horse droppings.

There was also a patch of flattened grass where a man had lain for a considerable period of time. She stood with the basket on her arm, worried at the thought that somebody had been camped there all night and knew where they were living. She felt that it had to be someone who had followed Josh rather than coming upon the place by accident.

She went back to the cabin, and when the men returned, told them what she had discovered. They started packing whatever the gig would carry; hauling the three hogs aboard, chasing the poultry round until they were all encased in a large basket, and loading everything else that could be carried.

They set out before noon, leaving behind the little place that had been a safe home, and heading north for another hideout. Ma Bladon fretted at having to leave so much behind, but there was no choice. The watcher could be heading for Pyke's Crossing. The marshal could even be on his way with a posse. Flight was the only sensible option.

The place they were headed for was a small cluster of mining cabins that had originally stood on a creek that had dried up when a rock fall had cut off the water supply. The area had been deserted for years because the nearest water was now a mile or more away. The Bladons would have to manage as best they could, riding out each day to replenish their drinking needs. Ma

Bladon drove the gig, cursing her menfolk for their incompetence, and blaming herself for being part of such a family.

They settled into one of the bigger cabins. The roof had to be repaired, and all the spiders and scorpions cleared out to make it livable. But it was large. More spacious than the one they had just left, and with cracked glass still in the two windows. There was no stove and Will had to build one of stone and a few iron rails that were lying around. He complained bitterly at having to work, but his wife's voice was shrill and demanding. He and his two sons buckled down and did what they were told.

Once they were as comfortable as could be managed in their new surroundings, Will set off to meet Josh Abbot to discuss the next bank job. He left his sons behind, feeling that one man would be less conspicuous than three.

It was a long journey to Josh's little

cabin on the fringes of Tombstone. The scruffy old man lived there amid smelly squalour and was troubled by nobody. He did a few odd jobs for local ladies, had been known to help with gardening chores, and was a regular supporter of the local saloons.

Will rode at a steady pace, halting each night at whatever water source existed, and taking the mule with him to carry food and anything else he might need.

He reached his brother-in-law's place in the mid-morning of a hot, dry day, and was glad of the meal that the other man placed before him.

'I didn't expect you so soon,' Josh said as they drank coffee on either side of the rickety table. 'You must be mighty eager to make a few dollars.'

Will looked round the filthy cabin with disgust plainly written on his face. He eyed the spiders uncertainly and could see a small roach clinging to the edge of the cot in which Josh had spent the night.

'You look as if you need a few dollars yourself,' he said gruffly.

The other man laughed. 'Don't let this place fool you, man,' Josh chuckled. 'Nobody bothers an old tramp like me. They feel sorry and offer me a drink — or a job. Now then, let's get down to the reason you're here.'

He felt in the pocket of his greasy waistcoat and produced a folded sheet of paper. When he spread it out on the table, it was clearly the roughly drawn plan of a small town that had one main street with back lanes radiating from it.

'Now, this is Maverton,' he said proudly. 'It's twenty miles south-west of Tucson and money for the quarry company wages bill is due in there next Friday. The company men will be in town the following Tuesday to collect it so that they can get it to their office and have the wage packets made up for the end of the week. You gotta take that bank on Monday morning.'

'Sounds easy, the way you say it,' Will

grunted. 'They got one of them bell things?'

'They sure as hell have,' the other man chuckled, 'and if you ain't got your wits about you, it poses a real man-size problem.'

'So tell me the bad news. All I need is a wasted journey.'

Josh grinned and scratched his armpit luxuriously.

'It ain't wasted, fella. If you just do as I tell you and don't go gettin' fancy ideas of your own, you'll clear that bank of every cent its got. But it means workin' at it. Not rushin' in and shootin' wild like some liquored-up Indians.'

Will stirred uneasily in his chair. 'Get on with it, fella,' he snarled. 'I came a long way to hear this, and you gotta earn the money you'll be takin' off us.'

'They got an alarm bell, just like the bank in Pyke's Crossing. And you have to stop it ringing without anybody bein' the wiser that it's been tampered with.

And that's where the hard work comes in.'

He pointed to the map with a grubby finger.

'This here bank is made of brick and the bell is on the roof, at the back of the building. The rope runs just over the edge of the roof, through a pulley, and then down a gap between the two layers of brick. Y'see what that means?'

Will did not see what it meant but he hated to show his ignorance.

'You tell me,' he snapped. 'That's how you're earnin' your money.'

'You can't get at the rope anywhere outside the building. Except from the roof. It's got to be cut before it passes down between the brickwork. That means that somebody has to get up to the edge of the roof to do the job. They've got to climb up, cut the rope, and secure the end that goes into the bank. That way there's no slack and everything appears normal.'

Will snorted. 'How in hell can we get on the roof?' he demanded. 'Are we expected to carry ladders into town and set them up against the wall of the bank? That'll sure make us noticeable folk.'

Josh grinned. 'But that's exactly what you're gonna do,' he said cheerfully. 'You're goin' into town with ladders, and set 'em up against the wall of the bank. Just like you said.'

6

Maverton lay between two ranges of rocky outcrops that for the last ten years had been supplying building material for the larger towns. A railroad spur ran to the quarry to take the stone off on the long journey round the southern parts of the territory. There was talk of extending the track to Maverton itself, but nobody felt that the town was worth it. Except the inhabitants, and they did not have the money to pay for the work.

They did have the telegraph though, and mighty proud they were of the advance in communication that it gave them. They also had a weekly stage that brought the latest newspapers. And they had a bank.

It was there on the main street, right between the marshal's office and a gun store. It was splendidly built in reddish brick with a stone frontage. Maverton was proud of its bank. It had the latest big-town safe and an alarm system that had never been beaten despite three attempts in the last couple of years. They had caught all the bandits involved and enjoyed a really good hanging each time with plenty of hymns and a general feeling of piety.

Sunday was a quiet day and the young fellow in the telegraph office was half asleep when a stranger entered and took off his dusty hat politely.

'We got here as soon as we could,' he said as he wiped the sweat from his face. 'You got any idea where the break is?'

Billy Crawford looked at him blankly. 'What break are you talkin' about?' he asked in a puzzled voice.

'The break in your line, fella,' the young man said earnestly. 'Ain't you been tryin' to use the telegraph in the last hour or so?'

Billy shook his head. 'Ain't had no need to,' he said. 'Is the line down?'

'Sure is. Somewhere between here and the main junction. We got a report this mornin' and my boss is a real stickler for movin' fast. He reckons the telegraph is just about the most important thing in his life. We've checked every pole from Derby Township to here, so we figure the break is somewhere in your town or beyond towards Merino. I hope as how we strike lucky soon. It's as hot as hell out there and this old bastard is one mighty slave driver.'

Billy Crawford got up and crossed to the window. A small buckboard stood outside the office. It was drawn by two mules and had a painted sign on the side that told the world that it was the property of the telegraph company. An older man sat on the sprung seat with another young fellow at his side. There were ladders and some tool kits on the small wagon with large coils of wire lying amid a string of insulators.

'You got a duplex system here, I see,' Matt Bladon said as he looked over the telegraph equipment on the bench.

'Mighty good system, and I don't see nothin' wrong with it.'

He spoke with authority and nodded his head as if agreeing with himself.

'I don't know what system it is, fella,' Billy Crawford admitted cheerfully. 'All I know is that I presses the key and deals with the messages. You reckon you can fix it?'

'We usually do,' Matt said confidently. 'A line down somewhere or a broken insulator. Some drunks even shoot at the insulators just for the fun of it. They're our biggest problem.'

Billy nodded agreement. 'I heard tell of them goings-on,' he opined knowledgeably. 'Drunken cowpokes tryin' to show off their speed on the draw. It ain't right, and that's a fact.'

'It sure ain't, but we'll soon have you fixed up proper, with any luck. I'll get back now to the boss and tell him there ain't no fault in here. We'll check the wires behind the building and then work out towards Merino.'

Billy Crawford resumed his seat and

left young Matt Bladon to join Nick and their father at the wagon. They drove it round to the back of the telegraph office to put a ladder up against the wooden wall. Matt climbed it confidently to make a detailed check on the wiring there. The fact that he did not know what he was doing, did not matter. Nobody was taking any notice, and if they had, they would be as ignorant as he was.

The ladder was gradually moved along the buildings until it was propped against the rear wall of the bank. Matt climbed up again while Nick held the ladder secure for him. The young man could see the bell that sat on the peak of the roof in a small turret of green-painted wood. A rope came down the sloping roof and passed over a metal pulley before vanishing just under the eaves between the layers of brick that made up the wall.

Matt looked down at his brother and nodded. He reached into the tool bag that was slung over his shoulder, took out a pair of cutters, and applied them to the rope. It parted easily and he held on to the end nearest the wall very carefully in case it fell between the bricks beyond his reach.

He now used a hammer and nail to pierce the rope and pin it to the brick-work just under the eaves. If anybody in the bank placed a testing foot on the pedal behind the counter, the tension would still be there. To complete his work, he wrapped some cotton round the rope that lay on the roof and secured it to the nail that held the other piece. It would not now flap around in the wind and draw attention to the severance.

'All done,' he said as he climbed down the ladder. 'Let's get the hell out before somebody wakes up.'

Nick nodded agreement and the two men carried the ladder back to the rig. Will took the reins and they drove out of town at a dignified pace.

'I reckon we can take that bank in the morning,' Will chuckled as he drove. 'They'll never know what in hell hit 'em. Josh has earned his money for once in his useless life.'

'Stop at the next telegraph pole,' Matt said in a quiet voice.

'What the hell for? The play-actin' is over now.'

'Because I gotta connect up the wire again, Pa,' the young man explained patiently. 'If the telegraph don't work, they'll start wondering what we was doin' in Maverton.'

Will slowed down the rig. 'You got a head on them shoulders, fella,' he said proudly. 'Takin' after your pa.'

The ladder was unloaded again, Matt climbed the pole, and the wire was reconnected to the insulator while the other two watched.

'Well, that's that,' Will said as he whipped up the two mules again. 'We'll be rich folk this time tomorrow.'

★ ★ ★

Monday morning was a quiet time for folks in Maverton. The saloon was shut after a lively weekend, the preacher was catching up on his drinking after all the speechifying, and children were back at school with long faces and freshly washed necks.

When three men rode down the main street, past the closed jailhouse, and the mayor's office, nobody noticed. It was Will Bladon and his two sons. They did not tether their horses to the bank's hitching rail, but went on to the gun store and dismounted there. The three men glanced in the window, pointed out various shotguns to each other, and then strolled casually across the board-walk to the door of the bank.

There was hardly anybody about as they entered. The inside of the building was also quiet, with three clerks talking in a little group and one elderly man just coming away from the counter with a small bundle of banknotes in his hand. The place was bright and clean, with polished brasswork and a gilded mirror that was engraved with the name of the bank.

Everybody looked around at the entry of the three men. It was only a glance of mild interest until the guns were drawn and the four people realized that they were the target of a robbery. One of the clerks moved back to his position behind the counter. He was a short man, thickset and tough-looking. He placed both hands in sight on the polished top but Will Bladon grinned as he saw that the man's body was shaking slightly as he pressed the pedal beneath his foot to ring the alarm bell on the roof. There was no answering sound from outside.

'You can stop that, fella,' Will said cheerfully as he poked his Colt .44 under the man's nose. 'You ain't got no bell. We fixed it just like we'll fix you if you give any trouble. Now, just start fillin' up these bags with cash money while I go pay a visit to the boss man.'

Nick stayed near the door, keeping the room under his eye while he was also ready to deal with anybody who entered the bank. Matt pulled out three canvas bags from under his shirt and passed them across to the clerks. A wave from his gun started them opening the cash drawers with trembling fingers.

Will went across to the glass-panelled door that was painted with gold lettering to show that the office beyond was occupied by the manager. He entered quietly and surprised the stout man who sat behind a roll-top desk. The manager went pale when he found himself staring into the barrel of the Colt. He glanced uneasily at the large safe in the opposite wall and raised his hands slowly as Will shoved the gun under his button nose.

'Open it up, fella,' the robber said quietly, 'and you'll live to go home to your wife and kids. Just don't do anythin' silly. I ain't long on patience.'

'You won't get away with this,' the man muttered in a choked voice. 'We got law in this town.'

'Yeah, I know, but you ain't got no alarm bell. Listen, fella. It ain't ringing.'

The manager listened, sweat pouring down his pasty face. Everything was quiet except for the heaviness of his breathing. He rose slowly from the chair and took a bunch of keys from his pocket. Will stood behind him as the safe was unlocked and the heavy door pulled open. He handed the man a couple of bags and watched as they were filled with all the cash that could be seen.

'You won't get far,' the manager warned. 'The marshal's posse will hunt you down wherever you ride.'

'Yeah, I know, and I'm real scared. Now, just tie them bags up all neat and then go sit down again. I don't aim to hurt nobody, but I intend that nobody hurts me none, either. Just sit quiet and it'll soon be over.'

He crossed to the door and threw it open.

'Finished, boys?' he called.

The two men nodded with grins on their faces.

'Right. Bring 'em all in here.'

The clerks and two customers were herded into the manager's office. Will looked at the little old lady who had not been there when they entered the bank.

'Where did she come from?' he asked Nick.

'Walked in large as life, Pa,' the young man answered. 'I figured she had to stay. Didn't do no yellin' nor nothing. Real cool, she is.'

The old lady heard what was being said about her and gave a radiant and somewhat senile grin.

'Just another adventure, lads,' she said in a musical voice. 'I pioneered this country. Seen out two husbands, and lived through the war. What's a bank robbery after that?'

'What indeed, ma'am?' Will said gallantly. He waved his gun at the manager. 'Give the lady your chair, fella.'

He turned to Nick. 'Did you fasten the front door?' he asked.

'Yes, Pa. Hammer and nails, just like you said.'

'Do the same here then.'

Nick took a small hammer from under his shirt and drove a couple of nails firmly into the door between the office and the main part of the bank. Will opened the rear door which gave onto a short corridor and led to an alley.

'Now, I'll tell you what we're gonna do,' he said to the prisoners. 'This here window is high up and barred, so it ain't much good to you. We're leavin' by the back door and we're gonna nail up this one. You folks can start yellin' as soon as you like, but I figure it'll be some time before you're heard and set free.' He turned to his sons. 'Let's head out, lads. We're done here.'

The three men left by the rear door of the office and Nick used the hammer and nails to make sure that the others were trapped inside. This done, they emerged into the alley and walked round to the main street where their horses still waited patiently outside the gun store.

They mounted calmly and rode out

of town without anyone paying attention. Will even raised his hat to two ladies who passed on the boardwalk. They simpered at him and went on their way.

Once clear of Maverton, they speeded up and were soon on course for their new home. None of them had noticed that Mike Wade had watched every move of their neat little operation.

7

The money lay on the table. A pile of notes and a jumble of silver dollars that glowed under the candlelight. The smell of Ma Bladon's pipe was heavy on the warm air of the little room as they all stood admiring their cleverness.

'How much?' Will asked Matt.

'I reckon it as five thousand, six hundred dollars, Pa,' the young man said in an awe-struck voice. 'We really hit it this time, didn't we?'

'We sure did, son,' Will said proudly. 'And not a shot fired in the whole danged shindig.'

'I steered you right,' Josh Abbot said as he leaned forward and removed a bundle of notes from the table. 'One thousand dollars was what we said, plus the money I lent you to hire the rig and gear from Mickie Rourke. I'll give you one good bit of advice from an old-timer. Don't go spendin' too free and easy. It's the way to make folks suspicious.'

'We ain't fools,' Will snapped indignantly as he swept the rest into one of the canvas bags. 'Now, I reckon we could use a good meal and a few drinks to celebrate.'

Josh shook his head. 'Do it without me,' he said. 'I got a long way to go, and I need the rest of the daylight. Now, just remember — keep quiet and don't go spending. I'll be callin' on you again when I've set up another job. So don't go strayin' from the path of righteousness.'

He left a short time later, hunched in his saddle and heading north at a steady pace. Will did not pretend that he was not glad to see the back of his brother-in-law. He hated the air of experience and confidence which the other man possessed. Besides, Will had things to discuss with the family, and he did not want a man whom he considered an outsider to be listening to his future plans.

It was after supper, when it was dark outside and a few shots of whiskey had been consumed, that Will told the others what he had in mind.

'This place will do us for a while,' he said as he chewed on a wad of tobacco. 'Ma can go into town and buy a few things at a time. We can make it comfortable here, clear up some of the land, and have it look like we're runnin' a little homestead. Water's the problem, but we'll just have to make the trip to the creek every morning. It ain't as if we was goin' in for bathin' in the stuff.'

He caused a laugh and spat out a stream of juice at a passing roach.

'Now, I figure as how a thousand dollars is a mighty pile of money. I ain't sayin' that Josh didn't earn it, but it sure dug into our take, and he was safe at home while we was out workin' for it.'

'You wouldn't have a dollar to your name if it hadn't been for my brother,' Ma Bladon snorted in his defence. 'He knows how to go about these things. Listen to him and we can end up mighty rich folk.'

Will nodded hasty agreement. 'Sure, sure. I ain't arguin' against that, but now that we know how these banks operate, maybe we don't always need him around. One of us could go into town and sniff out the local bank. Save us a mint of money.'

He gazed round the table with a wily grin on his unshaven face. Ma Bladon looked doubtful and glanced at Matt for support. He was the brighter of her two sons, and she relied on his common sense.

'You got somethin' in mind, Pa?' the young man asked.

'Sure have, son,' Will grinned. 'The sweetest set-up known to man. We'll take the Pyke's Crossin' bank again.'

'Holy Moses!' Ma Bladon screeched. 'The last time you raided that bank, we ended up with just enough money to feed a dead coyote. And you got yo'self a hangin' set-up into the bargain. Ain't you the sense you was born with, Will Bladon?'

Her husband refused to be angered. He just grinned cheerfully and leaned forward across the table to take them all into his confidence.

'Figure it out for yourselves,' he said in a conspiratorial voice. 'We know all about that bell alarm this time. We go into town, all cleaned up like we was decent folk, check out how it's fitted up on that there roof, and then play the trick with the telegraph lines on them.'

'Pa, it won't work,' Matt said quietly. 'They'll soon have the news about how we operated in Maverton. Once they see the newspapers or somebody gets into town and tells the story, we won't have a chance.'

'That's why we gotta move fast. Before they hear about it,' Will insisted. 'We set out first thing in the morning. Nick goes along to this fella Rourke to borrow his rig again while Matt and me go straight to Pyke's Crossing. Matt scouts the place out while I wait outside town. Then we meet by that bluff where the river widens. We cut the telegraph line like before, go into town, and fix that bell good and proper. Then we ride in the next mornin' and take the bank for every cent they got.'

'I don't like it,' Ma Bladon said bluntly. 'Let's rest quiet and wait for what Josh turns up with.'

'I agree with Ma,' Matt said after a pause. 'Bein' caught in Pyke's Crossin' would be a hangin' job.'

'You gotta take risks if you aim to be rich in this world,' Will said firmly. 'Are you with me, Nick?'

The younger son nodded. 'Sure am, Pa,' he said eagerly. 'I votes we do it.'

'Well, I ain't so certain,' Ma Bladon muttered dubiously, 'but it could just work and it's now or never.'

★   ★   ★

Old Reg Willey was in the middle of receiving a message when the telegraph stopped working. He tried to send out a few signals, but there was nothing on the line. He scratched his head in puzzlement and then decided to go along to the stage office and tell them that he had lost connection with Fort Reed. It was dusk in Pyke's Crossing and lights were going on in the windows that fronted the main street.

Old Reg shuffled along to find that the office had already closed for the night. He hesitated for a moment and then crossed back to the marshal's office. The lawman was just lighting a brass lamp that stood on his desk. He blew out the Vesta as Reg entered.

'The line's down again, Marshal,' the old man said grumpily. 'Right in the middle of a message for the Fargo people.'

Bob Payne lowered the glass carefully over the flame and turned up the wick a little.

'Some drunk cowpoke again,' he said knowingly. 'Or maybe you got yourself another rockfall out Mantegna way. Ain't nothin' we can do. Get an early night's rest while you can, Reg. The chance don't come too often in your job.'

The old man cheered up a little. 'Might do just that,' he said. 'Could even take a drink or two in the saloon.'

He did exactly that, and was a few minutes late opening up the next morning. He had just settled down at his desk to play a hand of patience when Matt Bladon entered with a cheerful greeting and the same story he had used in Maverton. He was on his way round the back of the building a few minutes later, carrying a ladder and accompanied by his father and Nick.

It was easier than Maverton had been. The building was lower and made of adobe. The rope from the bell came further down the wall to enter through a hole specially drilled in the upper part of a window frame. It could almost have been reached from the ground. The job was done in a matter of minutes and Will was driving the rig out of town with an air of triumph.

There was one change in their plan. They were going to dump the rig, collect their horses, and return to Pyke's Crossing later the same day. They had decided on noon, when the children were home from school and everybody was busy with a meal. It would be a quick operation and Will Bladon was feeling proud of his planning.

★ ★ ★

They rode back into town when the sun was almost at its peak. The place was quiet with some of the stores closed and folks sitting down to eat. The three Bladons tethered their horses round the back of the bank and then walked up the narrow alley to the board walk where the front door of the building lay invitingly open against the heat of the day.

Will looked round the almost deserted street. He peered through the doorway, and then gave his sons a contented nod.

'No customers and only the two

clerks,' he said softly. 'Let's get it done and be out the back way before anybody wakes up.'

He led the way into the building and the two bank clerks found themselves facing his gun as he flung a couple of small bags on the counter and demanded that they hand over all the cash. The men quickly obeyed and it was easy to see that the older one was frantically moving his foot beneath the counter. His whole body shook as he pedalled the lever that should be ringing the bell.

Will just grinned and left his sons to it while he went through to the now familiar office where only a short time ago he had killed the previous manager.

The room was empty. The man had gone to lunch. Unfortunately for Will, he had also locked the safe and taken the keys with him. The bandit cursed vividly as he kicked the closed door of the large green monster. He stood uncertainly in front of it for a moment before going going back to the main part of the bank. His sons had already finished their part of the job. The front door was nailed up and they were ready to usher the two clerks into the manager's office.

'How much money you got there?' Will demanded angrily.

'Two or three hundred dollars, Pa,' Nick told him with a cheery grin. 'How about you?'

'Get them two fellas in here and let's move the hell out,' his father snapped.

The two brothers looked at each other before waving the clerks into the empty office. They saw the locked safe and Matt pulled a face at his brother. They asked their angry father no questions but hurriedly nailed up the door leading into the main part of the bank, and then left the office by the rear door, nailing that up after them. There was another room to cross. It was a dark, musty place and led directly to the back alley where their horses were tethered.

Matt opened the door and found himself staring into the barrels of two shotguns. He opened his mouth to warn the others, but was pushed roughly back into the room. Will and Nick had no chance. The guns were also pointed at them and Nick was carrying the money bags.

Marshal Payne's bulk filled the doorway, and it was his weight that had driven Matt back inside. Behind the marshal stood the slim figure of Mike Wade.

8

Will Bladon sat disconsolately on the narrow bunk of his small cell. His two sons were next door, sharing another cell and both lying stretched out on their uncomfortable beds to try and get some fitful sleep. The evening was warm with insects buzzing around the lamps in the marshal's office. He and Mike Wade sat on either side of the desk, contentedly drinking their coffee after a leisurely and substantial supper.

'You and me sure done a good job, young fella,' the marshal said happily. 'That reward is gonna go down nicely. You certain you're tellin' me the whole story?'

Mike grinned. 'I told you what you needed to know, Marshal,' he said quietly. 'And it caught them fellas neat as pie.'

'Yeah, it sure did at that.' Bob Payne

chuckled as he sipped the hot brew.

Will Bladon crossed to the bars of his cell.

'Hey, you fellas,' he interrupted. 'How in hell does it happen that you was waitin' for us? We didn't tell no one we was comin' to your town.'

'We got ways,' the marshal shouted back with massive dignity.

'You got informers,' Will insisted. 'I reckon as how someone's been tellin' tales. My no-good brother-in-law.'

'Hold it, Pa,' Matt yelled urgently. 'Keep your mouth shut.'

Marshal Payne winked at Mike before getting up from his chair and crossing to the bars.

'Your no-good brother-in-law, eh?' he mused as he stared at Will. 'Now, who would he be?'

'I was just mouthin' off,' the prisoner muttered. 'A fella gets a bit mad at bein' caught like this.'

'I can imagine, but has this fella got a name? Maybe we oughta be havin' a talk with him.'

'Uncle Josh don't know nothin' about it,' Nick shouted angrily.

Matt could be heard groaning at the way his father and brother were behaving.

'So now we have a name for him,' the marshal grinned. 'You'll be givin' me the rest of the family history next. Maybe he did turn you in, fella. We get told lots of things about folk like you. Before you cut our telegraph, we heard that you did the Maverton job. And you sure got away with plenty in that fly-blown little town. But we was waitin' for you. Uncle Josh was mighty informative.'

'That no-good bastard!' Will raged as he rattled the bars and cursed his brother-in-law.

Matt got up wearily from his cot and pushed Nick away from the door of their cell. He took his place so that he could almost see his father next door.

'Pa,' he said urgently, 'stop talkin' like that. You're makin' matters worse. Nobody in the family knew we was comin' here. That was the whole point.'

Will opened his mouth to say something, and then stood silently for a moment. He lowered his hands from the bars and slowly went back to the narrow cot.

'I was wrong,' he said in a low voice. 'Take no heed of a foolish old man.'

Marshal Payne signalled to Mike. 'Let's you and me take ourselves off for a drink while these fellas get some sleep, lad,' he said with a wink.

He led the way from the jailhouse and stalked heavily across the main street to the busy saloon. It was bright and cheery, with brass and copper lamps hanging from the ceiling while smaller ones stood in front of the gilt mirrors. A few men were playing cards, but most stood or sat with beer in front of them. The marshal was greeted as a hero and neither he nor Mike had to pay for their drinks.

When the fuss of their arrival had died down, the two men stood contentedly at the bar with glasses in their hands. The marshal leaned forward confidentially.

'Now, let me get all this straight for the judge, son,' he said slowly. 'You was here in town, havin' a drink, and you saw this suspicious-lookin' fella checkin' round the back of the bank. You followed him out to that canyon, and when the bank was robbed, you took me out there. I'm right so far?'

'Yes, Marshal.'

'And then it all went wrong. All we got was some two-cent rustlers. Better than nothing, I suppose, but no reward. So then you come back to Pyke's Crossin' lookin' for work, and you see these fellas again. Right?'

'Right, Marshal,' Mike agreed. 'I sees them with the rig, doin' some work on the telegraph lines. So I lays low, and comes round to your office. And a fine trap you set for them, Marshal.'

The lawman grinned. 'I did at that. They never stood a chance. And I'm right grateful to you, young fella. We'll get ourselves a real good hangin' outa this affair and folks will be buyin' me drinks till I retire in a couple of years time.'

'Will I have to tell my tale to the judge?' Mike asked.

'Bless you, no, lad,' the marshal said warmly. 'You'll be long gone before the trial comes up. I'll give all the evidence that's needed.'

The lawman put down his glass and felt in his waistcoat pocket. He took out a few banknotes and thrust them into the young man's shirt pocket.

'That's for you, son,' he said quietly. 'Fifty dollars. You can leave town in the mornin' and nobody will be askin' you any questions. I'll do all the talkin' in court.'

'The reward was two hundred, Marshal,' Mike said in a hard voice. 'We was goin' shares.'

The lawman grinned. 'Quite right, son, and that's your share. A man can go a long way with fifty dollars, and it's more money than you can earn in a month.'

Mike Wade put down his glass and stepped away from the bar counter. His hand was going down towards his gun and the lawman's grin disappeared.

'Look behind you, fella,' he warned. 'I got two deputies back there and they won't be missin' your carcass at that distance. I reckon you should go right now, get on your horse, and quit town before I regret my generosity. Don't wait till morning.'

Mike glanced over his shoulder to see that two of the men who had been playing a hand of cards were now standing up. Their deputy badges were clear in the lamplight. Mike shrugged, finished his beer, and walked slowly from the saloon. The two deputies followed.

Marshal Payne watched from the window as Mike tightened the girth on his black gelding and swung himself into the saddle. The two deputies were standing in the doorway of the saloon, waiting for further orders. The marshal joined them.

'Kill that fella when you get him well outa town,' he said in a low voice.

The two men looked at each other.

'What's in it for us?' one asked.

'The fifty dollars I've just given him. Now, get goin' before he has a chance to outrun you.'

They nodded and mounted their own animals. The lawman watched while the little group headed out of town towards the north. He smiled as he turned back to finish his drink and see who would buy him another. He had not bothered to mention that news had come through on the repaired telegraph line that the reward was now another thousand dollars. It had been offered by the bank in Maverton.

★ ★ ★

Mike rode slowly. The two deputies were a few yards behind him, one on each flank of his horse. He had already made a shrewd guess that he was going to be killed when they were out of sight and sound of Pyke's Crossing. He slowed down a little more and let them come alongside.

'Are you fellas gettin' a share of the rewards?' he asked.

'We get paid to do our job,' one of the men answered. 'Rewards are the marshal's business.'

He paused for a moment and then rode closer to Mike. Their legs touched as he leaned over in the saddle.

'You said rewards, fella,' he challenged. 'There's only one reward. Two hundred dollars from the mayor.'

Mike shook his head. 'Two rewards,' he said as he looked straight at the man's dark face. 'Your marshal knows by now that the bank at Maverton was robbed by the same gang. Maverton are offering a thousand dollars. It's worth pickin' up, and that's the reason you weren't involved in nabbin' them Bladon fellas. Your marshal ain't the sharin' type.'

'And how much money did he give you?' the other man asked.

'Twenty dollars,' Mike said coolly. 'And told me to get the hell outa town. I reckon you're here to take it back. Will he let you keep any of it?'

'He said he gave you fifty dollars.'

'Maybe he thought you wouldn't kill a man for twenty.'

The men on either side of Mike eyed each other across his body. He could sense their uncertainty. The fellow on the right was still close to Mike, and their horses were almost rubbing flanks. Mike slid his foot from the stirrup and twisted it so that the spur stuck out towards the other man's horse. He looked up at the scudding clouds and waited for a few paces until the half-moon was suddenly covered as the night darkened.

The spur jabbed out brutally and the horse reared with a strangled cry as it shied away and stumbled in an effort to regain its balance. The man on its back cursed as he struggled with the reins. Both hands automatically grabbed for them as he slid awkwardly in the saddle.

Mike drew his gun and turned on the other rider. The man saw what was coming, tried to swing his horse round, while at the same time, going for his own gun.

It was Mike who fired first. The flash lit up the night and the rider lurched from the saddle, dropping his Colt as he plunged to the ground. His horse galloped off, raising a pale dust against the half-moon that now shone through the clouds again.

The other deputy had now got control of his animal. It was still fighting the bit as he pulled his gun from the holster. He heard the cocking of Mike's Colt as he did so, and changed his mind. His colleague was rolling on the ground and the deputy had no wish to join him. He spurred his mount savagely and galloped off in pursuit of the loose horse.

Mike Wade looked down at the man he had shot. The deputy was quiet now, lying on his side with the gun a few yards away. Mike patted the neck of his slightly trembling mount.

'Easy, boy,' he whispered. 'It was just a bit of shootin' between honest lawmen and a stray drifter. But I reckon we'd better head out before the marshal comes lookin' to add me to his list of hangings.'

9

Pyke's Crossing was in a state of excitement. They had not had an important trial and a triple hanging for years. Not since the days of silver and gold mining. The local judge, sobered for the occasion, was made to understand that Maverton also had an interest in the affair and would be sending someone along to sit in and make sure that justice was done. Justice meant a hanging. Nobody doubted that.

The marshal was still the town hero and the trial would make him even more popular. The recent loss of a deputy was hardly noticed. These things happened all the time and the lawman had let it be known that his two brave assistants had been pursuing potential rustlers when it happened. The last thing he wanted was for folks to know what really occurred.

The gallows was being erected at the end of the main street, just a dozen yards from the burial ground. It was an elaborate structure, built of good timber that was supplied by a company owned by the mayor. The hangman would be on his way very shortly. He had been telegraphed and a fee arranged. That had also been organized by the mayor. The First Citizen likewise made sure that the saloons were well stocked with extra beer and whiskey for the festive occasion. After all he owned them as well as the small hotel.

And while all this was going on, Ma Bladon waited in the distant cabin, wondering what had gone wrong and where her men were spending their time. She thought at first that they might have been off to some other town, celebrating their good fortune. Then she began to worry. They had been gone too long. Ma Bladon decided to go to Pyke's Crossing.

It was a journey of nearly two

wearisome days. Her mule pulled the little rig with maddening slowness across the uneven trail. She made camp wherever she could and was glad to see the buildings of the little town as she came round a stand of tall cholla cacti at the bottom of a long slope.

She had her story ready. She was an old widow woman with a little farm, and was coming in to Pyke's Crossing for a few essential supplies. She would be vague about things if anybody bothered to enquire, but Ma Bladon knew from experience that a woman like her was just taken for granted. Only people who had money or carried guns were looked upon with curiosity. She carried a gun, but not where anybody was likely to see it.

She did not at first notice the gallows. It was just out of sight at the far end of the main street, and she stopped her rig at the hardware store. The town seemed quiet enough and she put a feed bag on the mule before walking along the street to have a look at the bank and the marshal's office.

Everything appeared normal. The bank was open with people moving in and out, while a deputy sat on the stoop of the jailhouse reading a newspaper. It was only when she reached the grain store, which was on a bend, that the gallows loomed into view.

It gave her a start and she almost let out a little cry of pain. It was a tall structure, well built, with steps leading up to it. There was a long beam and three ropes hung from it. They moved slightly in the breeze as though heralding things to come.

She could now see the burial ground beyond and managed to control her emotions as she glanced round to rest her eyes on a food store that looked clean and inviting. She walked across and entered the sweet-smelling building. Another woman was just leaving with a full canvas shopping bag, and she nodded pleasantly to Ma Bladon as they passed each other.

The fat man behind the counter was

a cheerful soul who welcomed his new customer and was happy to exchange gossip as she made a few purchases.

'You seem to be gettin' ready for a hanging, I see,' Ma Bladon said casually as she sampled some bilberries. 'How did that come about? Rustlers?'

'Bless you, no, Ma'am,' the store-keeper answered in a loud, throaty voice. 'We got ourselves three bank robbers. Tried raidin' this town twice, they did, but the marshal got 'em dead to rights.'

'Clever man,' Ma Bladon said dryly. 'When's the hanging?'

'Well, the stage is due in today or tomorrow, and they reckon that the hangman will be on it. They've already booked him in at the hotel, so I'm told. Next day bein' the Sabbath, and all of us God-fearin' folk, they'll be doin' it on Monday. You figure to stay for it, ma'am?'

Ma Bladon thought about it as she sucked the fruit.

'I might do that,' she said. 'Ain't seen

a good hangin' for years. And ain't never seen three of 'em go together.'

The man nodded eagerly. 'That's how most folk feel about it, ma'am. This town is gonna be buzzin' come Monday.'

'I take it that the trial's already over?' she asked.

'Didn't last more than an hour,' the man assured her. 'Never was no doubt about the verdict. Them fellas was caught right in the bank. Took 'em without a shot bein' fired.'

'Well, I reckon Monday is a day I'm lookin' forward to,' Ma Bladon said with a smile.

She left town shortly afterwards and made camp by a small stream amid a grove of trees. She had taken a walk round Pyke's Crossing before leaving, noting each building and where the corrals were located. The cell windows were too high up and too small to be a means of escape. There were at least two lawmen around the place, and the jail-house was substantially built. She needed time to work out what to do. As she fretted over the problem at her little campsite Ma Bladon had not the faintest idea that every move she made was noted by a silent watcher.

★ ★ ★

The stage arrived quite early the next day. Only a few passengers alighted, and among them was the man everybody had been waiting for. The hangman and his assistant were met by the mayor, taken to the hotel, and treated to free drinks at the bar. After their kit was stowed, they went across to have a look at the gallows. The eminent visitor nodded his approval, tested the new-fangled trapdoor, and then retired with the mayoral party for another round of drinks.

Nobody took any notice of the neat little man who followed the party to the hotel, booked in quietly, and went to his room to unpack the large and heavy carpet bag he carried. He was quite elderly, with neat side whiskers, a dark suit and suede waistcoat, neat boots, and a gold chain across his stomach. A businessman of some sort, and of no interest in a town looking forward to a good hanging in a few days time.

The little man tidied himself up, took a couple of drinks at the bar, and then walked slowly along to the bank. He handed an engraved business card to one of the clerks, and waited patiently for the manager to emerge from his office.

Milford Christy was a large man, florid of feature and with the strong smell of tobacco and cologne wafting around him. He was a smiling man, and now beamed at his visitor as he shook hands and ushered the little man into the back office. He closed the door carefully, ushered the man to a chair, and brought out the best whiskey. As he sat down to share a drink, the smile vanished from his face.

'You've heard what happened?' he asked anxiously. 'I couldn't make it out.

It's not as we arranged at all.'

Major Codron shook his head and waved a deprecating hand.

'My dear fellow,' he said calmly, 'it was nothing to do with me. Everything has gone wrong through the behaviour of some foolish people who decided to try and tackle the same bank twice. That's what comes of helping one's kin. There is little gratitude in the world, my friend. They tried to work without me. They tried to cut me out.'

'Well, now they'll hang for it,' the manager snorted.

'And quite right too,' the major agreed. 'Indeed, were they not kin, I would be saying good riddance to a parcel of dishonest fools. Unfortunately, I will have a widowed sister on my hands. There is simply no justice in this life.'

The manager nodded glumly. 'How much did Ned get out of the Maverton affair?' he asked with sudden eagerness.

'I'm not sure but I reckon to there being eleven thousand or so in the safe.

Will Bladon took five thousand, six hundred, so he said. I reckon your brother pocketed about the same.'

Milford Christy sighed heavily. 'And we were hoping for a similar arrangement here,' he said without much hope.

The major shrugged. 'I was on my way when I heard the news. It was too late to turn back, but as I see it now, things will have to be allowed to quieten down for a while. I have another town in mind, but with this lot due for a hanging, it could take months to find another team to help us.'

'I'm surprised you don't still work with the Scanlon boys,' the bank manager said reproachfully.

'I wish I could, but Wally has made so much money out of it, that he decided to marry and settle down to an honest life. As for that brother of his, he took to drink and got himself shot in a brawl. That's why I used Will Bladon and his two sons. Guts enough to do the jobs but too stupid to know what the real game was. However, that's come to no good. The main thing is that I've brought what you need. And damned heavy they were to carry all this way.'

'Will they fit?' The voice was eager.

'If you measured up properly. But remember this, we can't do anything in Pyke's Crossing for at least a few months. Just be patient and you'll get your share without any danger.'

The dapper little man stood up to go. He shook hands with the manager and headed for the door.

'I'll be back tomorrow,' he said. 'They're in my carpet bag and all you have to do is to fit them and wait for things to quieten down. I'll send a message through when to expect a raid, and then it's up to you.'

Milford Christy nodded agreement.

'I'll do exactly as you say,' he assured the visitor. 'Are you staying in town for the hanging?'

'I've no choice unless I can hire a rig of some sort. If anybody gets curious about me, put it around that I'm thinking of investing in a local timber company. See you at the hanging.'

'Won't Will Bladon recognize you?'

Josh Abbot, now Major Codron, smiled a little.

'When he's up on that gallows, he'll have more to worry about than me,' he said. 'Besides, the man he knows, and the man you know, look quite different.'

Once back on the main street, Josh walked sedately along towards his hotel. There was a woman outside a drapery store across the way. She was taking the nosebag off a scruffy mule that was hitched to a small rig. He recognized his sister and hurriedly drew a large bandanna to blow his nose. She was too engaged in what she was doing to notice the little man who escaped into the hotel without being spotted.

★ ★ ★

Ma Bladon sat in front of the fire and smoked her pipe. She listened listlessly to the noises of the night as she

112

watched the moths skipping high above the flames. She had only the vaguest idea about how she would manage to save her men from the gallows. Her thoughts flitted from one plan to another, but without help of some sort, there seemed to be little that she could do.

The noise was slight, but her instincts were those of a woman always alert to danger. She reached for the shotgun at her side and aimed it at the shadow that loomed out of the darkness.

'Don't shoot, lady,' a voice called out cheerfully. 'I don't mean you any harm, and I ain't lookin' for trouble.'

'Then what the hell is you doin' here, fella?' she bawled.

'I'm here to help you arrange a jail break.'

10

Monday morning promised to be a hot day. The sky was cloudless and there was no wind. Pyke's Crossing was almost in a festive mood. The children were off school, the stores closed up after a couple of hours, and the preacher put on his best black coat. He had decided that a couple of Mr Sankey's hymns would do nicely, and had been practising his singing since early morning.

Three rough wooden caskets were laid out behind the scaffold. The mortician pestered the mayor for a better price, while the hangman and his assistant ate hearty breakfasts at the expense of the town. The three prisoners seemed to be the only ones not enjoying the day.

Marshal Payne brought them good breakfasts from the hotel across the street. He made extra coffee that smelled sweet and strong, and while they ate, he talked of events to come. When he finally paused for breath, Matt Bladon pushed his mug through the bars for more coffee.

'What time is it gonna be, Marshal?' he asked.

'Eleven of the clock, boy,' the lawman answered cheerfully. 'We usually do it earlier, but seein' as how there's three of you, a lotta folks want to come into town from round about. They gotta do the chores first before they leave home though. That sorta delays things. You understand?'

Matt nodded and managed a slight smile.

'We ain't complainin' none, Marshal,' he said. 'You gotta be considerate to folks.'

'My point exactly, son.'

Will Bladon sighed heavily as he leaned back on his bunk. He still did not blame himself for making a mess of things. They were all against him. That was the trouble. Life was unfair. He wondered where Josh was, and where Maggie was right now. There was a rare moment of compassion as he thought of his wife's distress at losing her family.

He did not know that she was less than a hundred yards away. Ma Bladon had driven into town almost as dawn was breaking over the dry hills. She left her rig in a gulley out of sight of the buildings and walked into the main street just as the stores were closing so that the owners could go to the hanging. People were all moving in one direction and nobody was paying any attention to one plainly dressed woman who carried a canvas shopping bag and seemed to be part of the scenery.

She stood on the edge of the crowd as they gathered round the scaffold. The preacher was hurrying around his flock, telling them what hymns he had chosen and to await his signals. Then he scuttled off to the jailhouse for a few drinks with the various officials of the town.

The hangman's assistant tested the ropes that had been left out all night. He made sure that they were properly stretched, ready for use. He also took a final glance at the mechanics of the new-fangled trapdoor and checked carefully that everything was in order.

The jailhouse was busy when Ma Bladon detached herself from the crowd and walked down a side lane until she was at the back porch of the hardware store. She glanced around, and seeing nobody, tried the door. It was not even locked. She gave a tight smile and entered the building. There was a living room first, neat and clean-smelling, with a large clock on the wall. She passed through to a store-room that smelled of wax and tallow, and then she stepped through another door into the store itself.

Sheer experience made her check the cash drawer first. There was money there and she pocketed it before looking around. What she wanted was under-neath the counter. It was a large barrel of lamp oil. A small tin hung by a wire under the brass tap and she smiled as she removed it to turn on the stiff faucet to start flooding the floor with the liquid.

While the barrel was emptying, she went to the window and peered carefully out at the main street. She could not see the gallows from where she stood, but the open door of the jailhouse was plainly visible. There were a group of men standing there, and she nodded her satisfaction before igniting the bundle of rags she took from her bag. The flames shot up as she threw them on to the flooded planks.

Ma Bladon retired quietly the way she had entered and went back to join the large number of women who were getting ready to sing about meeting at the river or the ninety and nine who did not stray from the fold. She could still remember the words, but did not intend to stay for the performance. If her plans went right, there would not be a performance.

It was a man who gave the alarm. He had been standing in the doorway of the jailhouse when a plume of smoke caught his eye. As he shouted to those around him, there was a tremendous crash as the windows of the hardware store burst with the heat and spattered the street with shards of glass. A gust of vivid flame shot from both windows to be smothered by thick smoke that curled into the still air and raised screams from the assembled women.

Ma Bladon watched carefully as the rush started towards the store while the mayor and the marshal tried to organize some sort of rescue plan. Buckets were called for and attempts made to form chains from the water troughs. There were also horses and carts to be removed from the scene of danger, while other buildings had to be protected from the flames.

Nobody took any notice of one woman slipping down a side lane and walking hurriedly towards the edge of town. Ma Bladon reached her rig, took the bundles of dry brushwood that lay in it, and tied them to the rear of the vehicle by a long piece of rope. She climbed up on the seat and began driving slowly towards a spot where she could see the southern edge of the town. And there she waited.

The marshal and his deputy worked wonders on the main street. They soon had a regular supply of water from the troughs and from a pump outside the feed store. Men and women alike were helping while the children ran around in delight at everything that was happening.

Mike Wade tethered his horse on the rails of a corral behind the jailhouse. He had three other animals in tow. All were saddled, and after he dismounted, he checked their cinches. There was nobody around as he walked up the back steps of the marshal's office and tried the door. It was unlocked and he stepped quietly into the corridor that led to the front of the building.

He opened the second door carefully.

It squeaked a little but nobody heard it. Everyone had gone to the fire and he was able to enter the room and remove the keys from the desk where he had seen the marshal stow them the day the Bladon family were arrested.

It was Matt who spotted him first. He came to the bars and was almost going to say something when he realized the need to keep quiet. Mike opened the cells and stood aside to let the three men come out. He pointed to the gun rack and waited while they armed themselves. It was Matt who recognized him.

'I know you, fella,' he said in a hoarse whisper. 'You was with the marshal the day we was caught.'

Will Bladon peered closely at their young rescuer.

'I do believe you're right, son,' he said angrily. 'What in hell is you playin' at, lad?'

'There ain't time to argue right now,' Mike snapped. 'Let's get the hell out before they know what's happening.

There are horses outside. All you have to do is to ride to wherever you feel safe. The black gelding is mine, so keep your hands off it.'

'You helped that marshal,' Will snapped as he checked the shotgun to see if it was loaded.

'He deputized me 'cos his own men were busy some place else. I didn't know what it was all about. Now get movin' while you've got a chance. And do it quietly.'

The four men went back down the corridor and out the rear door. They climbed on their horses and set off with Mike leading. Will Bladon caught up on his left flank and leaned over in the saddle.

'Why you doin' this, fella?' he asked suspiciously. 'We ain't got no money.'

'The marshal owes me,' Mike said tersely. 'I was supposed to get half the reward for helpin' him arrest some desperate bank robbers. Then he tried to have me killed. He owes me, and I owe him.'

Will Bladon nodded. 'That makes sense,' he muttered. 'That fire back there. You started that?'

'Your wife did,' Mike grinned. 'She's one hell of a woman.'

'Ain't that a fact? Where is she now?'

'She's waitin' on the edge of town with her rig. When she sees us headin' south, she's gonna make a dust trail up to the north. Then she'll stow her rig amid some trees and let the chase go wild and far. She said that she'll meet you at home. Wherever that is.'

Will nodded. 'And what do you get outa this, fella?' he asked.

'Well, I make that marshal look real foolish, for one thing,' Mike said slowly. 'You robbed his bank twice, so he tells me. And he still can't hold you in his jail. He'll be one right angry man when he finds you gone.'

'You can swear to that,' Will chuckled. 'And what are you aimin' to do after this?'

There was a slight edge to his voice. He did not trust the young man and was ready to use the shotgun that lay across the saddle.

'I aim to leave you when we reach those trees,' Mike Wade said quietly. 'I still got a lot to settle with that marshal fella and his deputy.'

Will nodded. He understood revenge.

'Then I'll thank you for what you did,' he said, 'and wish you luck.'

He turned in the saddle to see if there was any sign of pursuit. The trail was empty and there was no trace of dust in the still air. The four men rode in silence until the line of trees was reached at the base of the hills. Then Mike waved a hand in farewell and turned off to the west. The three Bladon men watched him go before entering the wooded area and making their way along the foothills towards their hideout.

★　★　★

They reached home safely after two days of travel and were joined a day later by Ma Bladon. She had some harsh words for them, but all her swearing and threats were taken in good spirit. They were safe again, and that was what mattered.

She threw a handful of money on the table and then emptied her shopping bag on top of the coins.

'I reckon I got more out of Pyke's Crossin' than you great jackrabbits ever did,' she snapped as she displayed her loot from the hardware store.

There were bundles of tallow candles, two scrubbing brushes, a couple of mop heads, and a coil of hemp that was tangled up with an assortment of soap bars, lamp wicks, and cutlery.

Will Bladon picked up a candle in disgust.

'Why the hell didn't you get wax candles?' he complained in an effort to re-assert his authority. 'They don't smell like these things.'

'If you want fancy candles,' Ma Bladon snarled, 'go back and collect them yo'self.'

She flung one of the scrub brushes at

him and the whole argument ended with them enjoying their meal and a few drinks from the corn mash jar. Will looked round the room as they all sat back, replete and safe again.

'I reckon life ain't all that bad,' he said in a contented voice. 'We got food and shelter, a few dollars, and plenty of chances to make more. Them folks back in Pyke's Crossin' must be goin' around with pretty long faces right now.'

They were. The mayor was furious; the marshal was threatened with dismissal, and the whole town smelled of wet, smouldering wood. Soot had settled everywhere, and only a few uprights remained of the hardware store.

One man was smiling though. The bank manager had been delighted to hear that the Bladon gang had escaped a hanging. He had his own plans for them.

11

Marshal Payne sat glumly at his worn desk. The patience cards were laid out in front of him but he was in no mood to play. A fly buzzed around his head and the office was heating up under the early-morning sun. His coffee had gone cold as he gazed blankly at the opposite wall.

Three weeks had passed and the Bladons were still at large. The escape had cost the town dear in repairs, the hangman's fee, and the loss of prestige in the eyes of all the folks around. The mayor and the councilmen had berated the marshal for leaving his prisoners unattended. He had no defence, but it was only his sound organization that had saved Pyke's Crossing from even worse damage as the sparks flew in the dry air. He got no thanks for that, and he knew that he could not afford another mistake.

He breathed a heavy sigh as he sipped the cold coffee. It tasted foul and he got out of his creaking chair to pour another one. Still clutching the mug, he crossed to the window and looked out on the main street. The storekeepers were brushing their stoops, the noise of hammers was coming from the smithy, and two young lads were rushing to lessons just as the last echoes of the schoolma'am's bell died away.

The marshal opened the door and flung the cold drink into the dusty street. He stood for a moment, letting the slight breeze tickle his face, when something suddenly occured to him. There were people standing outside the bank, and it was closed.

He gave a curse as he hurried back into the office, strapped on his gunbelt, and walked down the street with as calm a stride as he could muster. His mouth was dry and he could feel the heavy beating of his heart. More trouble at the bank was the last thing he could afford.

'What's happenin' here?' he asked one of the storekeepers who was talking to an elderly lady. 'Why ain't the bank open?'

'That's what we want to know,' the man snapped. 'I need change for the store and Milton Christy is near to half an hour late. That ain't no way to run a business.'

The marshal looked uneasily around. 'Has anyone gone to his house?' he asked.

Somebody told him that the two clerks had gone round there a few minutes ago. The group waited anxiously for something to happen and the marshal found himself sweating. He wanted to rush round to the banker's house, but could not make any move that might appear undignified.

One of the clerks suddenly came into sight from around the corner of a side lane. He was an elderly man, gasping for breath and red in the face from unaccustomed exertion. He came towards the group, saw the marshal, and grabbed him by the arm.

'The bank's been robbed again, Marshal,' he said in a rasping voice. 'Mr and Mrs Christy is all tied up in their house. You'd better come round and see for yourself.'

Bob Payne struggled to stay calm. He turned to the crowd and told them in a loud but slightly shaky voice that they had better come back in half an hour or so. This done, he followed the clerk back towards the manager's large wooden-framed house behind the feed store. Some of the people began to trail along, determined not to miss anything of interest. The mayor and one of the councilmen appeared on the street, and much to the lawman's annoyance, they joined the little procession towards the bank manager's residence.

The front door was open, and while the marshal entered, the mayor used a restraining hand to stop anybody else going into the building. The marshal's deputy came along at that moment, and took over door-guarding duties while the First Citizen hurried inside to see what was happening.

Milford Christy was in the middle of the living room, his large figure clad in a white nightgown and his face pale and unshaven. He was rubbing his wrists while the other bank clerk fussed around. Mrs Christy was sitting in a large armchair having hysterics to which nobody paid any attention. Pieces of rope lay on the floor and two bandannas were draped over the back of one of the chairs. The little clerk quickly explained to the marshal and the mayor what he and his colleague had found when they arrived at the house.

'Mr and Mrs Christy was all tied up to the chairs, Marshal,' he blurted out tremulously. 'Mr Christy had knocked his chair over and was trying to bang on the floor with his feet. We could hear the noise when we got to the front door. I tried lookin' through the windows, but the blinds was down. So we went round the back. The door was open and Bert and me came in and found them.'

Marshal Payne looked around the expensively furnished room. Mrs Christy was also in her night attire and was now sipping some brandy that one of the clerks had poured out for her.

'So, what happened, Mr Christy?' the lawman asked tautly.

'Yes, Milford,' the mayor butted in, 'for God's sake tell us what the hell's been going on here.'

Milford Christy gave a heavy and slightly theatrical sigh as he took a sip from his own glass of brandy.

'My good lady wife and I were in bed,' he said quietly. 'It must have been about two in the morning.'

'Ten minutes after, dear,' Mrs Christy chimed in.

'As you say, dear. Well, I suddenly woke up to find a gun stuck at my head. It was those three fellas you were supposed to be hanging. They'd come back.'

'The Bladons?' The mayor's voice

rose to a shriek. 'Are you sure?'

'I was closer to them than I am to you, Mathew Willard, and they were threatening to kill my lady wife unless I handed over the keys to the bank.'

'And did you?' The marshal's voice was almost a whisper. He could see his job vanishing before the day was over.

Milford Christy shrugged his massive shoulders angrily.

'What choice did I have?' he snorted. 'They were threatening to kill us both. I gave them the keys, was tied up and gagged, and off they went. If you'll just give me time to dress, I'll go down to the bank and see what they've taken.'

He and his wife retired to their bedroom while the mayor turned his anger on the lawman. Their voices were raised so much that the people outside could hear every word that was being yelled. The bank manager took very little time on his wardrobe. He returned within a few minutes, neatly dressed but still unwashed and unshaven. He led the little procession through the back lane, onto the main street, and to the front door of the bank. A spare set of keys jangled in his massive fist.

Half the town was by this time thronging in front of the locked door. The other bank clerk brushed them aside to let Milford Christy mount the two wooden steps of the wide stoop to insert the keys and throw open the portal. The deputy again kept the crowd outside while only those immediately involved were allowed to enter.

The little group stood in the centre of the main room for a moment, looking carefully around. Nothing seemed to have been touched, and Milford Christy led the way to his own office and flung the door wide. A faint whiff of stale cigar smoke assaulted their nostrils as they crowded in behind him and stood in front of the large safe. It was locked, and the whole place appeared to be undisturbed.

Milford Christy slipped aside the polished brass cover and inserted a key with trembling hands. He pulled the massive door slowly back and they all peered into the safe. Save for a bundle of deeds and some ledgers, it was empty.

'Oh, my God!' the manager groaned as he walked slowly over to his desk and sat down heavily on the creaking chair.

'How much?' the mayor asked hoarsely.

'Fourteen thousand dollars,' Milford said in a faint voice. 'They've cleaned us out of every cent.'

The marshal opened his mouth to make the usual official boast of catching up with the bandits in no time at all. Then he felt it best not to say anything. It might only make matters worse.

It was one of the clerks who spoke.

'I'll tell folk that we'll be closed for the rest of the day,' he suggested quietly.

Milford Christy pulled himself together. 'Yes, do that, Mr Davis, and then we'll telegraph head office. In the meantime, perhaps some of our leading citizens can lend the bank a little ready cash so that business can be transacted. Folks need to have confidence.'

He looked around hopefully but the mayor and the three councilmen seemed to be suffering from some hearing defect. The manager breathed a heavy sigh and drew a notepad towards him so that he could compose the necessary message.

Marshal Payne examined the interior of the safe and then walked slowly to the rear door of the office. He opened it with a look of dour concentration as he moved out to the corridor that led to the rear door of the bank. It was locked, and he went back to get the keys from the manager.

After opening the door, he stood for a few moments glancing round at the blank walls of the surrounding buildings and the corral of five horses and a mule that lay a short distance away. There was a puzzled expression on his face when he re-entered the building.

'Well, what are you going to do about this?' the mayor demanded of him when they had both retired to the jailhouse to discuss the matter.

'Do you really believe the Bladons came back to do this job?' the marshal asked as he poured his best whiskey for the mayor. 'Do you reckon on them as bein' that crazy?'

The mayor took the drink and sipped it thankfully.

'What are you implying'?' he asked suspiciously. 'Are you suggesting that Milford Christy is some sort of thief?'

'He's a money lender, ain't he?'

Mathew Willard leaned forward in his chair.

'Milford's a respected man in banking,' he said, 'so you gotta be careful if you're making accusations. What have you in mind?'

'Well, Mr Mayor,' the marshal said slowly, 'I don't pretend to be no Pinkerton fella, but I do claim to havin' some common sense. Now, you take them ropes that was bindin' them. It was the sort of sisal stuff that a woman uses to hang her washin' on. Do you figure on the Bladons carryin' that around with them? Then there was the horses.'

'What about them?'

'Well, there would be three of them, and they had to be left somewhere. There ain't no sign of 'em bein' outside Milford Christy's house. Nor at the back of the bank. You can't leave three horses for any length of time without there's some droppings. And hoof prints. And there ain't neither.'

The mayor rubbed his chin uneasily. 'I see what you mean,' he conceded. 'So where would the money be?'

'Could be any place, and I reckon as how an educated fella like Christy ain't gonna have it in his house. There's another thing, too. That horse trough behind the bank leaves a pool of water that flows down the lane, and there's always a bit of mud about. I would have thought that if three fellas was movin' around out there in the dark, they'd go trailin' that mud into the bank.'

The mayor stood up and crossed to

the window. He stared into the street with a worried look on his face.

'We'll have to be careful about this, Bob,' he said quietly. 'I just telegraphed Tombstone that the Bladons have done it. We can't go accusing Milford Christy without some proof. Any ideas?'

The marshal shrugged. 'I reckon we just gotta keep an eye on our local money lender,' he said. 'Leave it to me.'

Mayor Willard left shortly after and Bob Payne sat at his desk with a thoughtful look on his face. He knew that the bank manager had stolen his own money. His experience as a lawman told him that everything about the robbery was wrong. Had things been normal, he would simply have kept quiet, had a sly word with Milford Christy, and received his share of the loot.

But things were different now. His job was in danger after losing the Bladon gang. He needed the mayor on his side, supporting him against those who wanted a new marshal. Fourteen thousand dollars was a lot of money to turn down though, and he had an idea that might just work in more ways than one.

★ ★ ★

Milford Christy had shaved and was smelling slightly of cologne when the marshal called on him an hour or so later. The big man was carrying a cigar in his large fist as he admitted the lawman into the comfort of his home. Mrs Christy could be heard cooking a meal in the kitchen as the two men sat down opposite each other in large leather chairs.

'And what can I do for you, Marshal?' the banker asked with solemn dignity.

'Well, it's about this robbery, Mr Christy,' the marshal said sadly. 'The mayor is actin' rather strangely and I need to talk to somebody like yourself. Somebody I know I can trust not to breathe a word.'

The big man looked interested and leaned forward.

'You think the mayor had something to do with the robbery?' he asked.

Bob Payne shook his head.

'Oh, no. Nothin' like that,' he said, 'but he don't seem to believe the Bladons are mixed up in it. Now, he's a thinkin' sorta man, just like you are. And plain folk like me don't go in for all these fancy ideas. If you say it was them Bladon fellas, that's good enough for me. And it would make sense. They got a grudge against this town; they know the layout, and they could reckon on us not expectin' 'em again. Well, the mayor don't go along with that.'

Milford Christy shifted uneasily in his seat.

'Then he must think I robbed my own bank,' he said slowly. 'That's an awful thing to suggest.'

'It is indeed, Mr Christy,' the marshal agreed, 'and that's why I'm here. He ain't come out and said you done it, but I reckon they're the lines he's thinkin' on. Now, as I see it, the bank will be sendin' it's own people along to investigate this business. They'll talk to everybody, and what the mayor says to them could be real important. I figure he'll be leadin' them on the wrong trail, and that won't help my job. I want them Bladon fellas, and that means travellin' and spending.'

The last word seemed to have a little more stress to it and Milford Christy was sensitive enough to see the way the conversation was going.

'And what would you be spending money on, Marshal?' he asked politely.

'Well, people like the Bladons have contacts all over. I'd have to go from town to town, askin' questions and slippin' a few dollars into the hands of folk who don't care none for law and order. Cash money is all that matters to some fellas when you need information. The mayor ain't goin' to authorize expenses if he thinks the case is already solved.'

'Yes, I see your point, Marshal,' the

banker nodded. 'I suppose that you'll find a trail to follow. Something that would prove that three men rode into town last night and went off again in a particular direction.'

'I reckon as how I'm a pretty good tracker,' Bob Payne said complacently. 'Findin' a trail would sure place everythin' on the Bladons.'

'And how much money do you reckon on needing for your work?'

'Oh, I figure that about five hundred dollars would guarantee results.'

A slight smile passed over the banker's face.

'That seems reasonable enough,' he said smoothly. 'I could finance your venture for the sake of the community. Wait here.'

He rose from the chair and left the room. The marshal could hear his steps on the stair and the creaking of floorboards overhead. When Milford Christy returned, his left hand held a bundle of dollar bills. He held them out to Bob Payne.

'Two hundred dollars, Marshal,' he said smoothly. 'That's all I have about me at the moment. If you should find a trail and prove that the robbery came from outside the town, there's another three hundred due to you. Perhaps more, as a sign of my gratitude for a job well done.'

The lawman got to his feet. His face had broken into a contented smile as he took the money and made for the door.

'I'll get some food together and set off in an hour or so,' he said. 'Too much wind or some rain in the night could spoil our chances. My deputy can look after the town and I'll tell the mayor that I'm gonna make a sweep of the area in the hope of pickin' up a trail.'

'I'm sure you will pick up a trail, Marshal.'

The two men shook hands and Milford Christy watched his visitor walk down the lane towards the jailhouse.

★ ★ ★

Bob Payne took a leisurely ride out of town. He was well equipped with food and drink. His bedding was carried by a patient mule and he intended to spend a couple of days in the quiet of the grassland before returning with a story that would suggest to the mayor and councilmen that perhaps the Bladon bunch had robbed the bank after all.

He prided himself on playing it both ways. He had warned the mayor that Milford Christy was the guilty party, but now he had the banker's money in his poke and there would soon be a reward offered. If he could pin it on the Bladon gang, Christy would pay more. Much more.

The marshal made camp quite early. He chose a noisy stream that ran clear over polished stones. The night was warm and the moon high as he settled down with a bottle of whiskey to digest a good meal. He made up his bed after a while and turned in. The noises of the night were a lullaby as flying insects circled the fire and threw dancing shadows on the low bushes around.

The horseman approached slowly. He could see the fire in the distance and was relieved that he had not lost the trail that Marshal Payne had left. The pursuer's horse was large, like himself, and as he tethered it to a small bush, his hand trembled. He reached for the saddle holster and took out the Winchester. There was already a cartridge in the barrel and he calculated the distance to the campfire and the sleeping man. It was all of one hundred yards. He was no marksman and would have to get a lot closer.

He crept as silently as he could over the uneven ground. The moon was still low and the shadows were long. He could see the curled form of his victim and the shotgun that lay alongside the recumbent lawman. The fire crackled and flared as some of the wood split and fell in a flurry of sparks. The man halted, waiting for the noise to cease as he reckoned that he was now within killing distance.

He levelled the Winchester and sighted squarely on the back of the sleeping man. The explosion rent the air and echoed in the night. The horses and mule strained at their tethers while the scurrying jackrabbits ran for cover. The body beneath the blanket shuddered before lying still again.

The big man breathed an audible sigh of relief and hurried across the open space to kneel beside the man he had just killed. He pulled back the blanket and found himself staring at a pile of cactus bushes.

'You don't get your two hundred dollars back that easy, fella,' the cheerful voice of Marshal Payne said from the shadows.

Milford Christy whipped round. He tried to pull down the lever of the carbine to eject the empty shell case and reload it.

'Drop it!' the lawman yelled as he levelled his Colt .44 at the flustered banker.

Christy had lost all sense of safety.

He ejected the case and the next cartridge sprang into place as the hammer came back ready to fire again.

Bob Payne pulled the trigger. The blast at short range caught the other man full in the chest. He fell backwards on top of the bedding and never moved again.

12

'You should never have shot him, you damned fool!'

Mayor Willard's face was purple with rage as he confronted the marshal in the jailhouse. The banker's corpse had been taken down from his horse and carried into the mortician's office. Bob Payne had entered Pyke's Crossing as a hero who had solved the bank robbery and brought the body of the thief back home.

'I had to shoot him,' the lawman whined in self-defence. 'He was tryin' to shoot me, for God's sake!'

'I don't give a damn about killing him, you mugwump!' the mayor yelled. 'But where the hell is the money he stole? I've got shares in that bank.'

'Lookit, Mr Mayor, I didn't have time to ask him. He was aimin' a Winchester at me. He'd already shot up my bedroll. It was kill or be killed.'

The mayor was silent for a moment.

'I guess you're right,' he conceded, 'but you and that dumb deputy of yours have searched the house and the bank. There's no money at either place. He's died without talking. And that damned wife of his refuses to open her mouth. I'll see she stands trial before this business is over.'

'I did the best I could,' the marshal said defensively. 'I laid a trap, and it worked.'

'Now, this trap you laid. Suppose you tell me all about it. I've got to explain this affair to the council.'

The marshal had his tale ready.

'I went along and told him that there was a suspicion that he'd robbed his own bank. Then I suggested that I might stumble on a trail leadin' outa town, if I had the finance. He jumped at it and gave me fifty dollars. I figured as how that was an admission that he was guilty as hell. He even hinted that I could make a false trail. Then I let him follow me. I reckoned he might want to shut me up in case I started askin' for more money as a regular thing. He was sure determined not to share the loot. He even bent over what he thought was my body in order to search it for the fifty dollars. That was when I got the drop on him.'

The mayor nodded thoughtfully.

'It sounds logical enough,' he said. 'And that reminds me. The fifty dollars is money that belongs to the bank. You can drop it into my office any time you're passing.'

The marshal nodded glumly. He had at least the consolation that he was still a hundred and fifty dollars to the good.

The mayor stared moodily into his drink.

'Fourteen thousand dollars is a hell of a lot to lose,' he said bitterly. 'Where the hell could he have put it?'

'We've searched everywhere. Even in the corral and his garden. We've damned near taken the place to pieces. Could he have passed it on to someone else?'

151

The mayor held out his glass for another drink.

'Who?' he asked. 'He's new to town and has no relatives close by. No, Bob, he's hidden that parcel of money somewhere in town, and we're going round with our eyes closed. It's a pity you had to kill him.'

The marshal opened his mouth to protest, but the mayor held up an admonishing hand.

'I know, I know,' he said. 'You had no choice. But them bank detective fellas are going to give us some strange looks, all the same.'

'Maybe the judge can give his wife a lighter sentence if she talks,' the marshal suggested hopefully.

'We could give it a try, but I've got a feeling that this is too big for our court. It could end up in Tombstone before some legal fella who don't operate our way. This is a story that's going to be in all the journals and put us well and truly on the map.'

'Will I be mentioned by name?' the

marshal asked with sudden hope.

The mayor sighed. 'Very likely,' he said, 'but they might just ask the same questions I've been putting. Why in hell did you shoot him before getting the money?'

The mayor left soon afterwards and the marshal settled down to hone his story of how he solved the bank robbery. If journalists arrived from Tombstone, he wanted to have everything right. They might even take one of those new-fangled photographs of him. He stroked his chin and wondered if he ought to start shaving more than twice a week.

His deputy entered the building to put an end to the lawman's dream of fame. Harry Ford was weary and wore a puzzled look on his lean, dark face.

'I been all round town, Marshal, just like you and the mayor said,' he grumbled as he poured himself some coffee, 'and there ain't been no strangers around who left after the robbery. There is one odd thing though.

There's a cowpoke proppin' up the bar of Mason's saloon. He ain't a local but I see him some place before. Just can't put a name to the fella, but he sure is familiar.'

'No ideas?'

'Didn't hear nothin' said about him. He's youngish, slim built, and well turned out. Got a black geldin' hitched to the rail. I seen that horse someplace too.'

The marshal frowned for a moment and then jumped to his feet.

'You only saw the fella at night,' he said angrily. 'That's why you don't recall him too well. But try thinkin' of bein' on the wrong end of his gun when he killed Luke Wilson.'

'The fella you gave the money to and sent Luke and me to get it back?'

'Sure as hell could be him. He had a black gelding.'

'I owe him for shootin' Luke,' the deputy said as he put down the coffee. 'I reckon to goin' right back and killin' him afore he leaves town.'

'No.' The marshal's voice was taut. 'We can't do anythin' that might make folks start talking. If that fella opens his mouth, we could be in a real mess. No, this has to be done all careful-like. We gotta ask ourselves some questions. For instance, why the hell has he come back to town?'

'To make trouble for us?'

The lawman nodded. 'Could be. He only has to speak to the mayor or a councilman, and you and me is lookin' for another job and maybe a spell in jail. We need to get him somewhere quiet. Where there ain't no witnesses. I think I'll go across to the saloon and take a drink with him.'

'Is that wise, Marshal?' the deputy asked fearfully. 'Do you want me to back you up?'

'I don't know whether it's wise, but you stay here and don't get trigger-happy. We gotta handle things quiet-like.'

Bob Payne took a deep breath and stalked across the street to the quieter of the two saloons where several cow ponies were tethered. The black gelding was still there and he stroked its flank as he stood for a moment to gather his thoughts before entering and facing the man he had tried to have killed.

Mike Wade was still at the bar. He had a half-empty beer glass in front of him and was wiping his mouth with the back of a bronzed hand as the marshal entered. Mike raised his glass in salute and the lawman went across to join him.

'You're just in time to buy me another drink, Marshal,' Mike said cheerfully. 'There's been a bit of excitement in this town since I was last here. Shot yourself a crooked money-lender, so they tell me.'

Bob Payne looked round the bar at the few customers. He knew all of them and nodded his greetings. The bartender filled Mike's glass and put another one in front of the lawman.

'What are you doin' back in town?' the marshal asked in as casual a voice as he could muster.

'Watchin' folk.'

'Watchin' folk? What the hell does that mean?'

'You tried to have me killed, Marshal,' Mike said softly. 'All for a few dollars. Now, that ain't a nice way to treat somebody who helped you make an arrest.'

'It was all a mistake, fella. Somebody told me tales about you, and I reckoned you was playin' some sorta double game. Let's forget about it. You killed Luke and scared the hell outa Harry. What folks is you watching?'

'Folks what rob banks. They tell me that the money wasn't found. Is that true?'

'Sure is.'

Mike took a long drink of his beer and wiped a hand across his mouth again. The marshal waited silently, not quite sure where the conversation was leading.

'If you was thinkin' of tryin' to kill me again,' Mike said slowly, 'you'd be makin' one hell of a mistake.'

'Would I now?'

'Yes. You see, I ain't aimin' to go runnin' to the mayor about what happened in the past. I'm no schoolboy tellin' tales on folk. And then again, I reckon to know where the bank's money might be.'

Marshal Payne glanced quickly round the room to make sure that nobody else heard the words.

'If you're playin' jokes, fella,' he said grimly, 'I ain't in the mood for it. So where is the money?'

Mike finished his beer and put down the glass.

'First things first. I killed Luke. Now I want the other fella.'

Bob Payne put down his own glass. His hand trembled as he did so and the glass rattled on the counter.

'You want to do a trade then?' he asked.

'That's right.'

'And then you'll kill me?'

Mike grinned and shook his head. 'Not unless you cross me a second time. There's rewards from Pyke's Crossin' and Maverton for the Bladon gang. Then there's another reward for this robbery when the money's recovered.'

'Well, we ain't got the Bladons, fella, in case you forgot that. They escaped.'

'I know where they are. Three rewards, marshal. Quite a lotta money.'

'And you want your cut?'

'No, I want it all.'

'Now, lookit!'

'No, Marshal, you do the looking. I take the rewards and you take the credit. That's why I'm not gonna kill you. You collect the money and pass it right over to me. It's a good trade as I see it. Your life must be worth more than a few thousand dollars.'

Bob Payne stood silently for a while. The young man's calm manner was frightening. He desperately wanted to kill the fellow, but it was too dangerous. If his own two deputies could not do it, then it was too much to risk in a saloon by himself. Maybe later.

'So where is the money?' he asked.

'Your deputy lives up at the north end of the town,' Mike said thoughtfully. 'I reckon you'll be sendin' him home soon. Maybe I'll meet him somewhere quiet and settle things between us. Then you and me can have another talk later in the week.'

Bob Payne raised his glass and took a slight sip.

'You're askin' me to send Harry into a trap, fella,' he said. 'He's been my deputy for ten years and I'd almost call him a friend. What sort of man would I be if I set him up for a killing?'

'Same sort you are now, Marshal. Go back to your office and send him home for the night. Make sure he's carryin' a gun, because I aim to meet him fair and square.'

The lawman nodded slowly. 'Well, I guess a fair fight ain't somethin' to complain about,' he said. 'But you and me has an understanding. I get the bank's money back and hang the Bladons, and you get the rewards. Then me and you don't go shootin' at each other. Right?'

Mike nodded. 'That's the deal.'

Bob Payne left the saloon a short time later and went back to his office. He let Harry go off for the night and sat uneasily behind his desk, not certain whether or not he was doing things the right way. He could still kill Mike Wade, claiming that he was one of the Bladon gang, and getting more praise from the town. Or he could wait quietly and see what happened. The bank had lost over fourteen thousand dollars. They would be grateful enough if the marshal recovered about twelve thousand — maybe eleven, or even ten. The crooked manager might have hidden the rest some place else. Who was to say otherwise.

Bob Payne nodded his head in slow satisfaction. He might lose the rewards, but there was another source of compensation. He decided to sit tight and just listen for the shots.

They were not long in coming.

★ ★ ★

Mike Wade left the saloon right after the departure of the marshal. He walked to the far end of town, stopping outside the rooming house where he had seen the deputy enter and leave on several occasions. He leaned over a hitching rail and waited patiently.

Harry Ford left the jailhouse, called into the saloon for a drink, and then made his way slowly up the main street and round the corner to the wooden-framed house where he lived. He did not see Mike at first. The moon was high but cast the shadow of a building across the silent figure that stood at the hitching rail.

'I've been waitin' for you,' Mike said softly.

The deputy halted and peered into the darkness. Then he realized who was standing in front of him.

'You're the fella what shot Luke,' he said grittily. 'I sure owe you one for that.'

He reached down for the gun at his side and drew it with dazzling speed. Mike reacted at the same moment, and two shots rang out in the echoing darkness of the back lane.

Mike staggered backwards as a bullet slashed across his right forearm. He almost dropped the gun before he could re-cock it for another shot. His opponent seemed to be unhit and Mike fired again. The bullet caught the man in the chest, but it did not matter. He was already slipping to the ground. Mike's first shot had been a fatal one.

There was a long silence as the thin drift of smoke dispersed in the breeze. Then people began to show themselves and stand around quietly as they waited for some explanation for what had happened. Mike did not try to leave. He waited for the marshal to appear.

Bob Payne was in no hurry. He came slowly round the corner, looked down at the body with scant interest, and then turned to the onlookers.

'Nothin' to get excited about, folks,'

he said cheerfully. 'This was just a little personal matter which don't concern us. A fair fight and the best man won. You can all go home and leave it to me and the mortician to deal with.'

Then he turned to Mike.

'Looks like you and me has a deal, fella,' he said. 'Go see the doctor about that arm.'

13

Josh Abbot was not a great reader of newspapers. They cost money and were full of nonsense about politicians and other crooked dealers. It was just that he was walking down Fremont Street to pick up his horse from the corrals behind the meat market and had to pass the offices of Tombstone's two journals.

Outside the premises of the *Tombstone Nugget* there were a couple of bundles of new editions ready for going on the stage to other towns. He glanced casually at what he could read between the folds of brown protective paper and rough twine. There was some sort of headline about a hold-up at Pyke's Crossing.

Josh stopped and looked closely at the top copy of the paper. Fourteen thousand dollars had been taken from the bank by the Bladon gang. They had tied up the manager and his wife, used the keys to open the safe, and cleared the place out.

The old man opened his mouth to use some vivid language but hastily remembered that he was in his Major Codron persona. He took a deep breath, went to buy a newspaper, and then walked with dignified restraint to where his horse was patiently waiting.

He read all the details in the privacy of his own home. The Bladons had done it again. Acted like a bunch of untamed polecats and were very likely trying to cheat him out of his cut. He flung the offending paper across the room before going to get the clothes that made Josh Abbot a smelly old nobody who could travel without hindrance. The Bladons were not putting anything over on him. He was going to collect his share or else.

It was only after he had set out on his long journey to their hideout that more news came in on the telegraph to the pair of newspaper offices in Fremont Street. The Bladons were not involved and the marshal of Pyke's Crossing had caught the real culprit after a shoot-out. The editor of the *Tombstone Nugget* was furious that he had already rushed the first story to press so that it would catch the next stage. The more cautious proprietor of the *Tombstone Epitaph* was now smiling triumphantly as he composed the columns for his edition. He would also stress that the *Epitaph* always got the story right, and did not rush to judgement.

★ ★ ★

Ma Bladon was trying to find out where the wandering poultry had been laying their eggs while Nick was repairing a jumble of worn harness at the door of the house. Will sat beside him, chewing tobacco and ignoring any suggestion from his wife that the hogs needed to be kept from the vegetable patch. Matt was noisily chopping wood behind the building.

It was peaceful, but money was running short again and Will was hoping that Josh might show up with another idea for making some. Besides, he had a quarrel with Josh. A stolen newspaper told him that eleven thousand dollars was missing from Maverton bank. Something was wrong about the deal.

He shaded his eyes against the falling sunlight as he studied the haze on the horizon. There was a horseman out there, coming towards the little home-stead and just clearing the wide spread of tall saguaro cactus that lay at the base of the arid slopes to the east.

'Matt!' he shouted as he got to his feet. 'Come over here and tell me what you can make of that rider. We can do without visitors right now. Your ma ain't got the family silver polished up.'

Matt put down the axe and came round the corner of the building to stand by his father and watch the distant plume of reddish dust.

'Just one rider, Pa,' he said.

'I can see that, damn it, but who the hell is it?'

The young man did not answer. He waited until he could get a better view.

'Not movin' fast,' he said as he shaded his eyes against the slanting rays of the sun. 'And he's gotta lot of stuff on the back of his horse. Come quite a ways, by the look of it.'

'He's makin' straight for this place,' Will muttered uneasily.

'Don't matter, Pa. We're harmless folk.'

Will thought about it for a moment.

'Yeah, I reckon you're right, son. If he's got any cash on him, maybe we could do ourselves some good.'

'Too risky, Pa. We gotta live round here for a while yet. Let's wait for Uncle Josh to come up with something.'

'It could be Josh,' Will said hopefully. 'We could sure do with the work. Go get the guns, just in case it ain't.'

Matt entered the house to emerge

with a shotgun and the old Winchester. Nick stood at one of the windows, holding another shotgun as all three waited for the approaching rider to be identified.

It was Josh Abbot. He was his usual scruffy self with streams of sweaty dust down his wrinkled face below an old hat that sat greasily on his head. He climbed down from the horse, spat his displeasure, and approached his brother-in-law with an angry scowl on his face.

'You gotta be one of the most stupid and crookedest fellas I ever seen in a long life,' he shouted hoarsely. 'You go raidin' Pyke's Crossin' without a word to me, get yourselves caught, and then have the almighty gall to go back again and make off with fourteen thousand dollars. I reckon you owe me, fella. You owe me one thousand dollars. We had a deal, God damn it!'

'Now, wait a minute, Josh,' Will Bladon protested, 'I never got no money outa that bank. Me and the boys figured as how we could raid it easy, seein' as how you'd told us about the alarm bell and all. And we was goin' to give you your share. But we walked right into a trap and was all due for a hangin' until Ma came along with some fella and got us clean away. There weren't no money, Josh. Not one bent cent.'

Josh spat again and came to stand within a few feet of his brother-in-law.

'I ain't talkin' about that bit of trickery,' he snarled. 'You got away with fourteen thousand dollars and I reckon as how you owe me a thousand of that.'

Will looked blankly at his two sons. Then back at Josh.

'What the hell is you talkin' about?' he demanded. 'I've told you, we was caught and jailed. They was goin' to hang us.'

'I ain't talkin' about that fool business,' Josh shouted. 'I'm talkin' about holdin' up the manager and his wife and usin' their keys to open up the place in the middle of the night. Now,

I'm tellin' you, fella, I gotta hand it to you for gall, but you ain't doin' me outa my share. So, let's have that thousand and I'll be on my way. We're not havin' any more dealings. I gotta trust the folks what work with me.'

Matt stepped forward and stood between the two angry men.

'We ain't been raidin' no bank since we escaped, Uncle Josh,' he said quietly. 'We been right here, bidin' our time until you set up another job. There ain't no money.'

Josh Abbot snorted his disgust.

'I can read a newspaper!' he yelled. 'The manager of that bank saw you. All three of you. He knows who robbed him. Fourteen thousand dollars you took, and I want my share.'

He glared at the three men who were shaking puzzled heads at him.

'You don't want to credit what's in the journals,' Will said defensively. 'We been here, just like Matt says. Maggie will be back soon. She'll tell you. If you don't believe us, you'll at least believe your own sister. And now I suggest you quietens down, loosen the belly band on that horse, and come in for a cup of coffee.'

Josh Abbot stood with a look of uncertainty on his face. He suddenly turned on his heel, loosened the girth of his tired animal, and then drew the Tombstone newspaper from his saddle-bag. He handed it wordlessly to Matt and watched while the young man read the words aloud to the others.

'It sure weren't us,' the young man said when he had finished. 'Somebody's made a mistake, Uncle Josh. Maybe this bank fella was playin' some game of his own.'

Josh Abbot opened his mouth to say something and then a sudden change came over his face. He stood silently for a moment, cursing under his breath as he tried to find new names to describe Milford Christy. He now saw the way the bank manager had used the escape of the Bladons to loot the safe and lay the blame on them. He had also cut

Josh Abbot out of his share. He walked silently into the cabin and sat down heavily while Nick poured a mug of coffee for him.

'I guess I'm wrong,' he said after he had taken a sip. 'It weren't like I thought it was. That fella!'

He checked himself and took some more coffee. He did not want his relatives to know what arrangements he had with various bank officials. It was Will Bladon who started being difficult now. He leaned over the table to confront Josh Abbot.

'Talkin' of newspapers,' he said grimly, 'Maggie picked one up last time she went into town for stores. It said that the bank we raided in Maverton lost eleven thousand dollars. After your cut, we only had about four and a half thousand. That don't make sense, Josh.'

'These bank fellas ain't honest, Will,' the other man explained carefully. 'They tell stories to the newspapers that make their bank look more important, or maybe they got some sort of insurance to claim. As you said earlier, you can't believe what you read in a newspaper.'

He looked hard at the three men.

'You ain't short of money already, are you?' he asked.

'We ain't got a lot,' Will admitted. 'Movin' out here and buyin' things for the house — you know how it is, Josh. We could use another job.'

Josh Abbot got up from his chair and wiped the dribbles of coffee from his chin.

'Not from me, fella,' he said flatly. 'Tell Maggie I called, and be careful what banks you raid in future.'

He headed for the door but was forced to turn when Will grabbed him by the shoulder.

'You ain't leavin' us in the lurch like that,' he stormed. 'We did a good job for you in Maverton and there's more than half the money gone astray. I reckon as how you and that bank fella was up to somethin' between you.'

Josh Abbot brushed away the offending grasp and lowered his right hand down towards his holster.

'Are you accusin' me of some trick like the one you was pullin' in Pyke's Crossing?' he asked angrily. ' 'Cos if you are, I'm takin' that from nobody. Kin or no kin.'

'You ain't leavin' here that easily, Josh Abbot. You owe us,' Will shouted as Matt tried to restrain him.

Before anybody could really interfere, Will Bladon had reached for the Colt at his side. He drew it angrily, pulling back the hammer with a noise that seemed loud in the small room. Matt grabbed his arm before he could pull the trigger, and the two men struggled for a moment.

Josh Abbot watched from the doorway. His own hand was curled round the butt of his pistol and the hammer was already back, ready to leap from the holster when required.

Will pushed his son away, lashing out furiously with his fist at the young man to send him reeling against the table. The coffee mugs tumbled over and one fell to the floor, shattering and spilling liquid across their boots. Will swung round to face his brother-in-law and tried to level the gun.

Josh drew and fired with dazzling speed. The sound was deafening, and made worse as Will staggered against the table which collapsed under his weight. One of the legs had given way and he sprawled across it to slide down to the floor. The Colt fell from his grasp as he sank against the over-turned piece of furniture and looked with glazing eyes at the man who had killed him.

Nick reached clumsily for his own gun, but was too late. His Uncle was already pointing a recocked pistol at both lads.

'I'm leaving,' he said firmly, 'and I'm right sorry it had to come to this. Take my advice, lads. Get yourselves honest work. You ain't cut out for bank robbin' and gun play. Tell your ma I'm sorry, but he didn't give me no choice.'

He backed out of the door, tightened the girth of his horse, and rode off while both brothers watched in dumb silence.

14

The two men rode in uneasy silence. Neither could trust the other. Mike Wade's forearm was still painful, and the bandage seemed to make matters worse. The doctor had done a good job of stitching but the flesh was now swollen and the wrapping too tight. Mike kept flexing his fingers as he rode, making sure that they were still working properly and would be able to pull a trigger when necessary.

The marshal kept sucking his teeth as he traveled on his large mare. He cast an occasional look at his companion, not quite certain how to behave, and very anxious to know where Milford Christy had hidden the money.

Mike was too smart to tell him. The first part of their deal had been completed. The deputy was dead, and now they were travelling north to carry out the next phase of his plan. They were going to capture the Bladon gang.

'How much further?' the marshal asked after a long period of silence.

'By about dusk today,' Mike answered shortly.

'I don't know that I'm doin' the right thing here,' the marshal complained. 'I ain't got no authority outside Pyke's Crossing, and we're two days' ride north of my patch right now.'

'If you get the Bladons, nobody's gonna complain,' Pike assured him. 'We can take 'em into Tombstone, collect the reward for the Maverton job, and leave them with Marshal Earp. Then I'll take you to the man who organized it all. When you have him, I'll tell you where the money is hidden. Then you'll collect more rewards. You're a lucky man, Marshal.'

'Not so lucky if you take all the money, fella. We need a better deal.'

'I ain't forgettin' you tried to kill me, Marshal. You got the only deal going.'

'That killin' business. That was just a

joke. Them fellas took me serious.'

'Sure they did, and I took them serious too.'

The lawman brushed some sweat from his upper lip.

'You sure you know where the money is?' he asked.

'I'm sure.'

Bob Payne grunted and they rode on in silence for a few more miles.

As they neared a ridge in the gathering dusk, Mike Wade reined in his horse and both men dismounted to creep forward and look down at a small cluster of ruined cabins that lay amid the slopes of parched grass and stones alongside a dried-up stream. A bluish plume of smoke arose from one of the bigger cabins and there were hens and a few hogs foraging around it. Some horses grazed in a large corral while a small gig was standing nearby. A pile of freshly cut timber lay against the wall of the building while washing fluttered on a line that ran from the cabin to a pole near the privy.

'That's where they are,' Mike said quietly. 'We'd best keep out of sight and see how many guns we're up against. You should have deputized a few men to come with us.'

'I don't share the credit any more than I share rewards,' the marshal growled.

He pointed to a small mound of newly turned earth and the wooden cross that sat at one end of it. Mike nodded to show that he had also seen it.

'One of them's dead,' he murmured.

They waited patiently and were eventually pretty certain that only the two sons and Ma Bladon were in residence. An oil lamp was lit inside the building as evening fell, and they could smell cooking. The slight sound of distant voices occasionally floated across the quietness of the night.

'When do we take them?' Mike asked.

'Well, I'm what you might call an experienced law officer,' Bob Payne said slowly, 'and there bein' only two of us, we ain't gonna take no chances. We wait until they're asleep, and then go in. And take my advice, boy. Don't give 'em time to pull a trigger. We go in shooting.'

'And the woman?'

'She'll be out the door fast as she can make it. We let her go. There ain't no point in burdenin' ourselves with a female on the way back to town. If we play this right, fella, we'll end up with two dead bank robbers. And that saves one hell of a lotta trouble for everybody. Agreed?'

Mike nodded. 'If you say so, Marshal.'

'Right. Then we wait until the light's been out a while, creep up on the place, and let fly with shotguns.'

They settled down to wait. Mike lay on his back, looking up at the scudding clouds as they flitted across the face of the moon and changed the shadows around the two men and their horses. He felt along the sandy gravel through which the shrivelled grasses pushed their yellowing fronds. A small pebble came within his grasp and he rolled over on his side to face the patient mounts.

He flicked the tiny stone at his horse and grinned as the animal jumped backwards, bumped into the other pony and set them both clattering their feet among the stones and dead foliage. The noise was loud in the stillness of the early night and he heard the door of the cabin open.

Marshal Payne was cursing softly as he saw Nick Bladon standing in the opening with a shotgun in his hands.

'I did hear something, Ma,' the young man said loudly as he looked around in the darkness. 'It was somewhere up on the ridge.'

Matt came to join him. He too carried a shotgun and both men made a perfect target silhouetted against the light of the oil lamp behind them.

'Get the Winchesters, quick,' the marshal snapped as he saw the chance of finishing things at a safe distance.

Mike did as he was told, and unholstered the rifles from both horses. He crept back to the ridge and the two men took careful aim at their targets below.

'Whatever spooked them horses sure did us a good turn, son,' Bob Payne chuckled. 'Give it to 'em now.'

Both men opened fire. Mike aimed carefully at Matt whom he considered the more mature of the two. His shot took the man high in the right shoulder and he dropped the shotgun as he staggered against the door frame. The marshal's shot missed its target but he quickly levered another cartridge into the barrel and fired again.

Nick fell to his knees, tried to recover, and managed to fire a wild blast with both barrels of the gun. The spread of shot went aimlessly into the ground a dozen yards away as he slipped forward on his face and lay still.

Matt had picked up his own shotgun and was trying to see who was shooting at them and where the enemy were located. He raised the weapon to his shoulder but another shot took him in the chest before he could pull the trigger. It was Mike's second bullet, fired from a kneeling position, and as fatal as the marshal's had been to the other brother.

'Well, I reckon as how that does for the Bladons,' the marshal said happily. 'Let's go down there and send the old woman on her way.'

'She'll be right glad to get the hell out,' Mike assured him. 'I'll bring the horses.'

He went back to where the animals were standing uneasily with their heads close together as though for comfort. He slipped his own Winchester back in the holster, took the reins, and led the horses slowly down the long slope towards the lighted cabin.

The marshal hurried along some fifty yards ahead, the rifle under his arm and his stride denoting the victor. He stopped at the doorway, bent over both bodies to make sure that they were dead, and then went boldly into the lighted cabin.

There was a loud explosion as the lawman framed the doorway with his bulk. He seemed to leap backwards, the Winchester flying from his grasp as both hands flailed the air. He turned, facing the way he had come, hands still spread as though appealing to Mike Wade. Then he slowly dropped in his tracks and crawled for a few feet before lying still.

Mike waited quietly, stroking the noses of the restless horses. He watched as Ma Bladon came out of the cabin. She carried a Colt pistol in each hand and looked around carefully. The moon was behind the fleeting clouds and Mike stood silently as she edged along the wall of the cabin to the corral where the horses were nervously moving around.

He was not sure whether or not she had noticed him in the darkness, but his lack of movement helped. She shoved one of the pistols in the folds of her skirt and placed the other one on the ground while she picked up a saddle from the rail of the corral. She had one of the animals harnessed and ready to go with expert ease. Mike grinned as she retrieved the gun and mounted the horse with all the assurance of a man. It was the first time he had ever seen a woman in a skirt and apron riding astride a horse. She dug in her heels, cursed the world and all its works in a loud voice, and galloped furiously off towards the north-west.

15

Ma Bladon rode furiously for the first few miles. She had seen the vague figure of a man leading two horses but had not recognized him against the scudding clouds and heavy shadows. Will was dead, her sons were dead, and she was too concerned with escaping the rest of the posse.

There was only one refuge for her, and that was with the man who had shot Will Bladon. She bore Josh Abbot no grudge. Her husband was always rash, eager to act without thought, and always sure that he was clever enough to get away with it. He should have known that Josh would not back down. Her sons had given her a fair report of the event and they had buried Will with as little fuss as possible. And now everything was going wrong. She was on her own with a journey of two days or more before she could find a new home with her brother.

She had no time for grief. The ride was a hard one. She had no food or water, and would have to be on the lookout for pursuers. Her only hope was that the posse would consider a woman not worth the chasing. That at least gave her some wry amusement. She was more dangerous than most men.

It was a weary rider who finally reached the little hut on the southern edge of Tombstone. Night had fallen and the temperature was dropping as she came upon the small cabin. There was no welcoming light and the door was closed. A small ridge of blown dirt covered the ground in front of it, making it clear that nobody had been in or out of the building for several days. There was no horse in the little corral and no smoke from the iron stove pipe.

She cursed as she got wearily down from her mount. The animal was as tired as she was and went straight for the small water trough before she could even unfasten its girth. She let it drink a little, moved it to the corral, and then felt in the pocket of her skirt for a gun. She did not intend to walk into any sort of trap.

The door opened easily enough with a loud squeal as the hinges raised their protest. A stench of stale hot air struck her like a solid wall as she entered the little cabin and felt around to get her bearings. She bumped into a table, found a little cot, and then reached an iron stove. She passed a questing hand over the table and discovered a candle stub that had been knocked over.

She felt in her pocket for the little brass Vesta box and struck a light. The candle sputtered to life and she looked around her new home.

'I've sure had some bad times,' she muttered, 'but this beats them all.'

There was a little cupboard on one wall with an oil lamp on top of it. She shook the lamp hopefully and found that some fuel still sloshed around its bottom. It added to the warmth and brightness of the place. There was also some bacon and coffee beans.

Meagre as it was, the meal was enjoyable and Ma Bladon slept on the cot, undisturbed by moths, spiders, and a scorpion that had taken up residence near the stove. Things looked a little better when she woke the next morning and had her first cup of hot coffee.

All she had to do now was to find out where her brother was. She stood in the doorway of the cabin and looked out at the various other buildings that lay between it and Tombstone. They were mostly small places like the one she occupied, but they were surrounded by hens and hogs, and had vegetables growing to feed the families. She decided against asking any questions. Josh would not like it, and Ma Bladon still feared that she might be hunted.

She went back inside and decided to have a proper clean-up of the cabin. The scorpion scuttled off at the first scraping of the table and chair as she moved them outside while she swept the floor. The window was opened to clear the air while she removed cobwebs and dirt from every corner. Maggie Bladon felt better for doing the work and brought in water to wash down the stove once all the embers were cleaned out of it.

It was then that she noticed something odd. There was a small mirror attached to the wall. It was a mottled piece of glass in a walnut frame, but still served its purpose. On a little shelf beneath it was a shaving bowl with soapy water still in it. A razor sat close by aside a shaving brush. Ma Bladon picked up the razor and opened it. Josh was not a man for shaving, any more than Will had been.

She cleaned up the mess and then started to improve the little cot. It was a wooden structure with filthy blankets and a pillow stuffed with straw. Roaches fled the scene as she worked and a small lizard ran up the wall to escape her activities.

The chest was under the cot. It was made of stout planks and almost as long as the cot with a tight-fitting lid. Ma Bladon pulled it forth and knelt in front of it for a moment. She had some slight qualms about nosing into her brother's affairs, but curiosity got the better of her.

'Jumpin' Jehosaphat!'

The words came out involuntarily as she stared at the contents. Whatever she had expected, it was not this.

The clothes were clean and neatly packed. There were freshly laundered shirts, black linen stocks, and two suits of town wear that had cost real money. Josh's old Army Colt lay on top in its holster. The bullet mould was there alongside a powder flask and a small tin box of percussion caps. She pulled out the suits and put them on the cot while she looked at what lay beneath. There were good quality leather boots and a large bottle of expensive cologne.

Ma Bladon sat thoughtfully in front of the assortment for a long time, and then put everything back as she had found it. She decided to make some enquiries after all. The neighbours might know something that could be useful.

Having no rig and no side-saddle, she felt that it would be best to walk abroad like some respectable widow woman. With a canvas bag on her arm and her clothes brushed as cleanly as possible, she set out after a midday meal.

There were no other women about as she passed the sprawling mass of small fields and cabins, but one elderly man was hoeing a plot of vegetables in front of his own little building. Ma Bladon decided to approach him.

'I'm Josh Abbot's sister,' she said cheerfully. 'Callin' on him unexpected-like, and I find he ain't at home. Do you know where he could be?'

The old man came over to the fence and leaned on it to look closely at her through screwed-up eyes. He was thin and stooped, his face lined and his nose large with purple veins criss-crossing it.

'Josh told me he had a sister,' he chuckled as he displayed one single tooth in the middle of his gums. 'Said she was a mighty fine woman, he did. I reckon as how he was right.'

'So where is the old devil?' Ma Bladon was in no mood for flattery.

'Well now, I reckon as how he's gone a'courting.'

The old man peered closer at Ma Bladon to see what her reaction might be. He was not disappointed.

'Courting!' she almost shouted. 'And what woman would be fool enough to look twice at him?'

'He's a mighty dapper fella when he's dressed up and shaved all neat-like. I clean up pretty well myself when I've a mind to. I could take you into town one night to one of them hymn-singin' shindigs the ladies like so much.'

Ma Bladon looked at him with a slight smile on her face.

'If ever I'm short of a bullet to shoot myself, I might just accept that offer,' she said. 'Tell me, don't folk round here

196

wonder why he suddenly changes the habits of a lifetime?'

The old man chuckled. 'They don't see him,' he said in a confidential whisper. 'He goes off at night. I'm the only one as knows about it.'

'And where in Tombstone would I be findin' this washed and shaved brother of mine?'

The old fellow shrugged. 'He never did tell me who the woman is he's a'courting. Real secretive sorta fella is Josh.'

'Well, I can't deny you've the right of it there.'

★ ★ ★

The fine house was just on the outskirts of Tombstone. It was fronted in red brick with sturdy wooden sides and a tiled roof. It even had cast iron gutters and barrels to hold rain water. There was a large front garden and a corral round the back that housed two fine riding horses and an old mule. A four-wheeled rig stood nearby, displaying a folding linen hood and well polished paintwork.

It was the house of a substantial citizen and Mike Wade grinned slightly as he tethered his mount at the whitened gate and walked slowly up the gravel path to the front door.

There was a slight delay after his rat-a-tat on the brass knocker and he waited patiently for the owner to admit him. It was a dapper, elderly man who opened the door. He sported a neat moustache and sideburns, wore a suede waistcoat that displayed a thick gold watch chain while a pair of gold-rimmed glasses adorned the end of his nose. His shirt was a dazzling white emphasized by the deep purple of his stock that housed a diamond pin.

He blinked at the visitor and raised an enquiring eyebrow.

'And what can I do for you, my dear sir?' he asked in a well-modulated voice.

'Major Codron?' Mike tipped a finger against his hat in polite salute.

'The same, young man. Late of the Army of the Confederacy. How can I help you?'

'Would you by any chance be related to Josh Abbot and the Bladon family?'

The pale blue eyes of the little man froze as though some veil had come down over them. He looked for a moment as though he would close the door, but then seemed to recover his poise a little.

'I think you have the wrong person,' he said softly. 'I don't recall knowing any of the names you mention.'

Major Codron was still calm but there was an alertness in his face as he held the half-open door firmly as though ready to slam it shut.

'Will Bladon and his sons are dead,' Mike said bluntly.

'His sons!' The words escaped the man before he could control himself. 'What about Maggie?'

'She killed the marshal of Pyke's Crossin' and got away.'

Josh Abbot realized that he had

admitted his relationship with the Bladons. He opened the door wider.

'You'd better come in,' he said as he looked around to see if the neighbours were prying behind their curtains.

Mike entered the wide hall and was ushered into a room on his right. It was a bright place, one wall lined with books and framed prints. There was a large mahogany table in the centre and comfortable-looking armchairs on either side of an empty fireplace.

Josh Abbot hesitated for a moment and then went to a cupboard to take out the whiskey bottle. He poured two drinks and handed one to Mike.

'How did it happen?' he asked.

'The marshal tracked them down and went along with a posse. Will was already dead and buried, but the two lads started shootin' and were both killed. That's about all there is to it.'

Josh nodded sadly. 'And you were in the posse, I take it?' he mused.

'Yes.'

'So how come you know about me?'

'That's a long story and it ain't important now,' Mike said coldly. 'But I do know somethin' that might interest you. It's about the money that Milford Christy stole.'

Josh Abbot's hand trembled as he held the glass. His voice took on a keen edge.

'You know where it is?' he asked.

'Yes. Interested?'

Josh swallowed the whiskey and licked his lips eagerly.

'I'm very interested,' he said, 'and I suppose you want a cut, fella.' He paused as a thought struck him. 'Why in hell are you here? You already know where he hid it, and you don't have to share with nobody.'

Mike grinned. 'Major Codron's grammar is beginnin' to slip a little,' he said. 'I need you because I can't get at it.'

'And I can? So where the hell is it?'

'Where you told him to hide it.'

Josh's mouth dropped open in dumb surprise and he took a turn around the room before coming to rest again in front of his visitor.

'Then he never had the sense to move it,' he muttered to himself. 'Of all the damned fools.'

'He never got a chance to move it,' Mike told him. 'Marshal Payne was too quick with a gun. So it's there for the taking.'

Josh looked at the young man and tried to assess his character.

'And why should I give you a cut?' he asked. 'I could kill you, clean as clean, and Major Codron is one respected man in these parts, let me tell you.'

'Mr Abbot, I'm pretty fast with a gun myself, and Marshal Payne lost two deputies by tryin' to twist me outa money. Fifty percent of that cash is better than a memorial stone to the late Major Codron.'

Josh scratched his chin. 'Well, son, you might have somethin' there,' he admitted with a grin. 'But I got a lot invested in this. How about sixty for me and forty for you.'

'I won't argue that point, and maybe

we can work together on some of your other jobs.'

Josh Abbot brightened up. 'That's a thought, young fella,' he said. 'With the Bladons dead, I'll sure need a new setup. And you got more sense than they ever had.'

'Is that a fact?'

It was a new voice. That of an angry woman, and the woman was Ma Bladon. She stood in the doorway that led to the kitchen, and threw her shopping bag on the nearest chair. Josh Abbot paled a little as he tried to put on a welcoming smile.

'Maggie, my dear sister,' he said in a beguiling tone, as he moved towards her.

'Don't you try the Old Southern Hero voice on me, fella,' she bawled. 'You shot my Will, and bad as he was, he was mine. And now I got no sons and no home. So who do I come lookin' for but my lovin' brother, and I figured on findin' you with a woman. But I bin listenin' at that door, and it looks to me like you've bin playin' us all for headless chickens.'

Josh gulped noisily and edged towards a rolltop desk that stood next to the window.

'How did you happen to find me, Maggie?' he asked. 'Tombstone is a pretty big town.'

'It ain't big enough to hide that horse of your'n. I just went around the corrals till I lit on it. Then it was just a matter of findin' the right house.'

She looked at Mike.

'And seein' you go in was all I needed to get the connection.'

Josh laughed uneasily as he leaned against the desk.

'Well, our ma didn't raise no foolish children,' he said. 'That's for sure.'

'Nor honest ones,' his sister agreed. 'And now I figure on havin' a reckonin' for all this. I want part of this money you've bin talkin' about.'

Mike glanced at Josh. 'I think that's fair enough,' he said quietly. 'Mrs Bladon's as deeply in this as we are.'

The older man nodded his head. 'Absolutely,' he said with false cheerfulness. 'We'll each give her a thousand dollars. Agreed?'

It was agreed and the atmosphere lightened. Some more whiskey was poured out in generous measure as they discussed the next steps in their plan to recover the money.

The loud knock on the front door came as a shock and the conversation died abruptly as all three looked at each other. Josh put down his glass and went to the window. He peered through the thick net curtains very carefully.

'The marshal and a deputy,' he said in a stricken voice. 'I'll have to let them in.'

He turned to look at his two companions. His eyes darted restlessly round the room as if for a means of escape.

'You're caught, Josh,' Mike told him as he pulled out a deputy's badge from his waistcoat pocket. The other man stared at it with mesmerized eyes while

Ma Bladon's right hand crept to the pocket in her skirt.

'I needed to be sure,' Mike told him, 'and the marshal's been watchin' the house since I arrived.'

Josh Abbot gave vent to one lurid curse and grabbed the edge of the ribbed covering that enclosed the top of the desk. He pushed it back a few inches and snatched the Colt .44 that lay already cocked on the green baize surface. He swung round with lightning speed and pulled the trigger.

Mike was still holding a whiskey glass in his left hand and the deputy's badge in the other. He was too slow in reacting, and it was Ma Bladon who came to the rescue. Without removing her hand from the pocket in her wide skirt, she faced her brother and her shot was almost an echo of his. But it was more accurate. Josh had fired wildly and missed Mike by several inches. His bullet hit the clock on the wall while his sister's shot, fired from the gun in her pocket, caught him in the chest.

He fell back against the desk and then slipped to the carpeted floor. Ma Bladon calmly smacked at her smouldering skirt with work-worn hands.

'Remember that I saved your life, young fella,' she said. 'I'll need a friend at my trial.'

Mike grinned. 'There's no lawman outside the back door, lady,' he told her. 'You just go out the way you came in, and you and me is quits.'

She needed no second telling and headed for the hallway with a curt nod of thanks. Mike watched her go and then opened the front door to admit Marshal Earp and his deputy. 'When you knocked on the door, he drew on me,' he said when they saw the body. 'I had to shoot him.'

Virgil Earp nodded. 'Saves a trial,' he said thankfully.

16

The mayor of Pyke's Crossing stood in the middle of the office. The new bank manager was with him and the third occupant was Mike Wade.

'Are you tellin' me, young fella,' the mayor demanded portentiously, 'that you can recover the money Milton Christy stole from us?'

'I think so, Mr Mayor,' Mike said in a humble voice. 'I've been watchin' all the people involved and was deputised by Marshal Earp in Tombstone to catch the man who planned it all.'

'And a good job you appear to have made of it there. So where is this money?'

Mike looked at the two stout, well-dressed men whose bulk seemed to fill the little room. He pointed to the safe.

'Josh Abbot used to size up bank

managers,' he explained with a sly glance at the present incumbent. 'He would approach them as a man who sold ideas for makin' their banks safer. One of his ideas was that they should have a hidin' place in their offices where most of the money would be stored. If the bank was raided, the bandits would only get what they could see. He was well paid for this.'

He glanced again at the new bank manager.

'If the money-lendin' fella seemed open to suggestions,' he went on, 'Josh would arrange for a gang he employed, to raid the bank. He would get a cut out of what they stole, and the manager would then claim that they got everything. Josh would collect another cut from him.'

The mayor's mouth fell open in reluctant admiration while the bank manager just stood looking slightly embarrassed.

'Then it all went wrong when the Bladons got away. Milford Christy staged another robbery, blamed it on them, and had all the money for himself. But he didn't have time to remove it from this office.'

'Then where the hell is it?' the mayor wailed. 'We've searched the place from top to bottom, and his house. It can't be here. He must have hidden it some other place and it'll never be found.'

'It's in the safe.'

The manager spoke for the first time. 'Don't be ridiculous, young man,' he said in a high-pitched voice. 'I use that safe every day.'

'Open it,' Mike ordered him.

The man reluctantly swung open the heavy door and stood aside while Mike removed the bags of coin and a few ledgers from the bottom of the safe. He pointed to the metal flooring.

'Underneath that,' he said.

He took out his clasp knife and drove the blade along the edge of the flooring. To the surprise of the other two men, the green painted metal base lifted in two parts and they were able to see a gap of a couple of inches between it and the real bottom of the safe. The false flooring had been supported on narrow wooden strips.

Bundles of banknotes lay neatly arranged in three rows. All the stolen money was in front of them.

'You can hide a lot of money in a space like that,' Mike said as he removed the two metal plates that Josh had installed after being supplied with the measurements by Milford Christy. That was why Major Codron's carpet bag had been so large and heavy.

'Well, if that don't beat all,' the mayor said as he slapped Mike on the back. 'You sure saved the reputation of this town, young fella. And there's a reward in it for you, as well. Got any plans for the future?'

Mike appeared to think about it for a moment.

'Well, I like Pyke's Crossing,' he said slowly. 'Folk are friendly and it would be a nice place to settle down if I can find a job.'

'Oh, I think we can take care of that,' the mayor said with a knowing wink. 'A young fella like you who saves the bank a lotta money and helps poor Marshal Payne deal with the Bladon gang, ain't gonna be short of a job around here. You're a handy fella with a gun, and I figure as how a man like you could be a pretty good law officer. We certainly need one at the moment.'

'Well, I'd sure be grateful for a deputy's badge, Mr Mayor.'

'Deputy nothing, young fella. I aim to make you marshal of Pyke's Crossing. What do you say to that?'

Mike smiled gratefully.

'I'd be right honoured to accept, Mr Mayor,' he said humbly.

He did not feel it necessary to tell the First Citizen that everything had worked out exactly as he had planned it from the beginning.

We do hope that you have enjoyed reading this large print book.

Did you know that all of our titles are available for purchase?

We publish a wide range of high quality large print books including:
Romances, Mysteries, Classics
General Fiction
Non Fiction and Westerns

Special interest titles available in large print are:
The Little Oxford Dictionary
Music Book, Song Book
Hymn Book, Service Book

Also available from us courtesy of Oxford University Press:
Young Readers' Dictionary
(large print edition)
Young Readers' Thesaurus
(large print edition)

For further information or a free brochure, please contact us at:
Ulverscroft Large Print Books Ltd.,
The Green, Bradgate Road, Anstey,
Leicester, LE7 7FU, England.
Tel: (00 44) **0116 236 4325**
Fax: (00 44) **0116 234 0205**

A few years after the Civil War, Lou Hollister returns to Texas, bearing the cruel scars of an enemy prison stockade. Once home, he thinks he can settle and cast off a beleaguered past. Instead, he finds a family without hope, and a ranch manipulated by Tusk Tollinger, the corrupt sheriff of Cottonwood County. Lou fights to regain his ranch, and when a great snowstorm surges in from the Sacramento Mountains, he must confront his tormentors from the past. Can he now wreak his final, bloody revenge?

HIGH STAKES SHOWDOWN

Mike Redmond

The placid work routine at the
Ferguson Ranch is abruptly shattered one afternoon when young
cattleman Matt Farrell discovers a
dead body on the range and
simultaneously finds himself at odds
with the foreman, McCoy, over the
favours of old Ferguson's feisty
daughter, Hetty. Now a breathless
sequence of events finds Farrell
braving a lynch mob, defending
himself in a brutal bare-knuckled
fight and facing death in a final
shootout in a spooky Arizona ghost
town . . .

THE GUN MASTER

Luther Chance

They lived in the shadow of a fear that grew by the hour, dreading the moment when their world would be destroyed by a torrent of looting and murder. And when that day finally dawned, the folk of Peppersville knew they would be standing alone against the notorious Drayton Gang. There was not a gun in town that could match the likes of the hard-bitten, hate-spitting raiders. But now it looked as if change was on the way with the arrival of the new schoolteacher, the mysterious McCreedy . . .